Keys to the Kingdom

Keys to the Kingdom

JACK O'CONNOR

PENGUIN
IRELAND

PENGUIN IRELAND

Published by the Penguin Group
Penguin Ireland, 25 St Stephen's Green, Dublin 2, Ireland
(a division of Penguin Books Ltd)
Penguin Books Ltd, 80 Strand, London WC2R ORL, England
Penguin Group (USA) Inc., 375 Hudson Street, New York, New York 10014, USA
Penguin Group (Australia), 250 Camberwell Road, Camberwell, Victoria 3124, Australia
(a division of Pearson Australia Group Pty Ltd)
Penguin Group (Canada), 90 Eglinton Avenue East, Suite 700, Toronto, Ontario, Canada M4P 2Y3
(a division of Pearson Penguin Canada Inc.)
Penguin Books India Pvt Ltd, 11 Community Centre, Panchsheel Park, New Delhi – 110 017, India
Penguin Group (NZ), 67 Apollo Drive, Rosedale, North Shore 0632, New Zealand
(a division of Pearson New Zealand Ltd)
Penguin Books (South Africa) (Pty) Ltd, 24 Sturdee Avenue, Rosebank, Johannesburg 2196, South Africa

Penguin Books Ltd, Registered Offices: 80 Strand, London WC2R ORL, England

www.penguin.com

First published 2007

1

Copyright © Jack O'Connor, 2007

The moral right of the author has been asserted

Set in 12/14.75 pt Postscript Monotype Bembo
Typeset by Rowland Phototypesetting Ltd, Bury St Edmunds, Suffolk
Printed in Great Britain by Clays Ltd, St Ives plc

A CIP catalogue record for this book is available from the British Library

ISBN: 978-1-844-88153-6

This book is dedicated to my late mother, a remarkably resilient woman with an unbreakable spirit. Even though she was being taken to the church the night I was officially ratified as Kerry manager, I felt she was with me every step of the way.

PART ONE
Winter

I

Funerals, always funerals. A huge part of GAA life is the following of coffins into and out of churches. Tonight I was up in Lixnaw for Eamon Fitzmaurice's grandmother's removal to the church. There's still a little bit of tension between myself and Eamon. He is hurt over missing out last year, but Eamon is solid. He'll be fine. We'll be fine.

I spoke to Seamus Moynihan, too, about next year. Seamus is ticking away on his own. We'll see how he feels after Christmas.

It is the third week in October – the 19th, to be precise – and my re-appointment as Kerry manager was confirmed tonight also. No fanfare. Low key. Just like I wanted it to be. It's just a few weeks since we lost the 2005 All-Ireland final to Tyrone. We are still raw.

The coming year will be my third and last year as manager of the Kerry football team. How we do will determine how I am remembered. Tonight two years ago we were coping with another funeral. We were taking my own mother to the church for burial. At the same time on the same night I was being ratified as the brand-new boss of a county team which seemed to be reaching the end of its own natural life.

I'm not one for odd beliefs, but somehow my mother is tied in with all this. The Friday before last month's All-Ireland final I did what I always do on the weekend of a big match. I went up the valley to my father's house and had a cup of tea with him. Then I went on away up the hill, right up into the mists of Toorsaleen mountain, looking for the solitude that I knew would clear my head.

It's raw and desolate up there but it energizes me every time. I get my best notions going up the mountain. Toorsaleen: high field of the little sally trees. There's a road goes up there, like a scar in the rock, a tough, tough slog. From the top you look out across towards the beach at Rossbeigh or down the cliffs beneath you, down the rock and shale to the dark of Coomasatharn Lake. A lonely but beautiful spot. It's good for the soul, being up there.

I stayed a little too long on Toorsaleen and it was dusk that Friday night when I made it down to the graveyard beside the new chapel. I've been among the headstones there a hundred times at least, but in the darkness I couldn't find my own mother's grave.

Finally I had to come out the gate and go home, but it was in my head all weekend. Something wrong. The thought stayed in my head all weekend.

As it turned out, there was plenty wrong. We lost the All-Ireland final to Tyrone by the margin of a goal. We won nine out of twenty-four balls that we kicked to our full-forward line in the final and we turned over possession again and again. We were out-fought and out-thought by a tougher team. That sort of thing hurts in Kerry. It hurts me.

Football is different here. People say that about a lot of places, but in Kerry it is true. Football matters more here than it does any place else. It's bred into the bone, taught from the cradle. When we train in Killarney we do so with the stark grey buildings of St Finian's mental hospital looming over us. Johnny Culloty, my friend and selector, whose working life was spent in there, often points out that in a good year, when Kerry win the All-Ireland, admissions to the place go down. A bad year is a year when we don't win the All-Ireland. This was a bad year.

Being close doesn't cut it. Tyrone beat Kerry by seven points in the 2003 All-Ireland semi-final. Being within a score of them in an All-Ireland final two years later doesn't make a bit of difference. Progress doesn't count. In Kerry there's winning and nothing else, there's first place and nowhere. Last month Kerry lost. End of story.

A sore, hard ending, too. We lost to Tyrone as we had done in 2003. People in Kerry have one abiding image of the 2003 semi-final. Eoin Brosnan, our big strong forward, on the ground with the ball in his arms and eight Tyrone players converging on him like a posse. Mickey Harte, the Tyrone manager, is looking on in the background, wearing his usual poker face. That picture confirmed what Kerry people had suspected in 2002 when we lost to Armagh. Football, our game, was changing. We were being left behind.

So losing again to Tyrone last month cuts deep. We won the All-Ireland in 2004, my first year in charge. We got to the final and won it, having hardly broken a sweat, except for a tricky tangle with Limerick. Our journey didn't take us into the path of Armagh or Tyrone, though. We won, but deep down in our hearts in Kerry we don't feel as if that 2004 All-Ireland took football back for us. In a good year in Kerry we win the All-Ireland. In a great year we reclaim the All-Ireland in style or we retain it for the second or third or fourth year.

Losing to Tyrone is worse than losing to almost anybody else. Not that there's much history between us. That's the point. There's an arrogance to northern football which rubs Kerry people up the wrong way. They're flash and nouveau riche and full of it.

Add up the number of All-Ireland titles the Ulster counties have won and it's less than a third of Kerry's total, but northern teams advertise themselves well. They talk about how they did it, they go on and on about this theory and that practice as if they'd just split the atom. They build up a mythology about themselves. That doesn't sit well in Kerry, where a man with four All-Ireland medals would quietly defer to another man who has five.

If we lose a game I find it hard to look people in the eye when I walk on the street in Cahirciveen. They know. Everyone knows.

We stayed in Killarney on the night after the final, and so I didn't get home from the All-Ireland until the Tuesday night. By then I was struggling with flu but I sat down to watch the tape, with my sons Cian and Eanna beside me contributing the sort of observations all selectors would make if they had the gift of perfect hindsight. Shoulda, coulda, woulda. Bridie was in and out. I just watched, sort of numb. I knew that I was going to be watching this one again and again.

Next day I escaped to a house my sister-in-law, Mary O'Neill, owns, just outside Kenmare. It's my bolt-hole. I have a little routine when I'm there. Get up early. Go for a run in Rinn na gCos, a little spot down off the Park Hotel. Home again. Have a shower. A bit of breakfast. I wander off then to see what the papers are saying about us. Most managers pretend not to read the papers. I read them, looking for any tiny nugget, be it a lie or a careless word, that might give us an edge. The loss to Tyrone has been our first defeat in a championship game in two years, and in the aftermath people are generally positive towards us — apart from the usual suspects.

Starting nearest to home, one in particular is getting under my skin. Sean Counihan, a former Kerry selector, has had a bit to say in the local paper. After the All-Ireland, when we came home to Kerry on the Monday evening, Pascal Sheehy, the RTÉ reporter, stuck a microphone under my nose in Tralee. He asked me about the future and I gave a throwaway comment to the effect that if the decision had to be made now, I'd be going now. It got picked up, and Counihan implied that I'd said I was going in order to take the heat off myself after a defeat. Cheap shot.

Sean Counihan is remembered as one of the Kerry selectors who took Aodán MacGearailt off in Cork in 1999 when he had scored two goals. If Sean thinks I'm cutting and running to duck some heat, he obviously doesn't know the feeling or the man.

Anyway, I get stuck in to the old video. I need to be on my own to rationalize it. I need to write things down as I watch.

A few home truths come out every time I press the 'play' button. Where it happened for us and where it didn't happen.

One incident makes me sit up every time I watch it. Darragh Ó Sé, our *fear laidir* in midfield, is coming out with a ball in the first half, and Brian Dooher of Tyrone, who is at least two stone lighter and a foot shorter than Darragh, gets his body in the way and stops him. He just stops Darragh in his tracks. Then he slaps the ball out of Darragh's hands. A few seconds later the ball goes sailing over our bar.

I watch it again and again, saying to myself that Darragh should be trampling this fella, he should be swatting him away.

Our momentum just went after that. After a good start to the game we were in trouble. There were more ambushes, incidents where Seamus Moynihan was turned over, where Aidan O'Mahony was turned over. Bringing the ball out of defence we were especially vulnerable, and then when we got the ball out of defence we couldn't make it stick in the full-forward line.

The tape of the game is like a work schedule unfolding for me, setting out everything we'll need to do for 2006. Toughness will be the mantra for next season. We'll break tackles and we'll tackle hard. We'll tackle in the way that little Brian Dooher tackles Darragh Ó Sé every time I look at the screen. First though I have to go away and I have to actually learn how to coach the tackle. Genuinely I don't know how to do that. Tackling is something that was never heard of in Kerry, beyond telling a fella to go out there and not foul the man.

I'm from south Kerry, where maybe the purest football in the country is played. Tackling is like heckling a tenor during his solo. We like to see the skills of the game on display. We enjoy catching and kicking. Even here, though, you have to be pragmatic. You have to play football that will win matches.

We have to persuade ourselves that there's nothing morally wrong with tackling! This is the third big championship game we have lost in four years to hard-tackling northern teams. It shouldn't be a hard argument to win.

People around here won't like it. Johnny Culloty will understand, but he won't like it either. Johnny is a great voice for me to have in my ear, he knows the romance of Kerry football better than anyone. His word to me always is that we have to win and we have to win with a bit of style, Kerry style. Johnny, you might have to look the other way for a while.

Often during the week in Kenmare I found myself on the phone to the lads. I needed the solitude but I missed the contact too with the men who were suffering like I was suffering. Johnny Culloty, Ger O'Keeffe and Pat Flanagan. As a backroom team we've talked nothing but football for two years now. It's the heart of our friendship.

We talked for hours on the phone. Post-mortem stuff. We got this wrong. That wrong. We didn't follow through on that. We should have seen this coming. With the phone calls we energized each other as the week went on.

I rang the players, too. Darragh was one of the first. The rap on Darragh, which I have never agreed with, is that he doesn't perform in All-Ireland finals. As far as I'm concerned, Darragh marked Sean Cavanagh in the final and Sean Cavanagh didn't score. Darragh scored two points. He played well and was unlucky not to kick the equalizer late on. He was inches wide after his brother, Tomás, got the goal which gave us a little hope in the second half. I called Darragh and told him he'd had a great final, that there was another year in him.

It's not always smooth between Darragh and myself but we need each other. He's upbeat about his own performance and his own future. I'm glad. I replaced Darragh's uncle Páidí as manager of this team, and I know it took Darragh in particular a long time to buy into what I was trying to do.

Talking to the players, there's a feeling that in many ways we were right there with Tyrone. We know too that we lost not just to a great team but to men who hit a peak after a long, long summer when they did the hard yards and played ten games, finishing in September so battle-hardened that they were ready for anything. On the other hand we had cruised through the season, never leaving the comfort zone.

Tyrone were better on the day, but not a lot better. The players say to me again and again that they have more mileage in the tank and more hunger in their bellies. Speaking to players brings the energy back. They were down and out, but togetherness helped the rehabilitation. The reception we got back in Tralee and Killarney when we came home was surprisingly good for a beaten Kerry team. We had a good night out in the Gleneagle Hotel in Killarney.

Then we sobered up and tried to straighten ourselves up, and it hit us again.

The players I have spoken to are hurting badly but, like myself, when they look back on the night of the All-Ireland, at the words that were spoken and the promises made (I was a bit misty-eyed myself when I was up on my feet talking), they feel this story isn't finished yet. I'm proud of how they stuck together after the defeat, of the speech our young captain Declan O'Sullivan made. If there had been division or if heads had dropped, myself, Johnny, Ger and Pat would have been out the gate and up the *bóthar* long ago. The biggest job this past season was getting them off the training pitch and keeping them off it. We wanted to keep the sessions sharp and precise. They wanted more and more.

Some evenings in Kenmare I'd go for a few drinks and a meal with Tom O'Connor. Tom and I soldiered together as Kerry selectors back in 1997 (a good year, a very good year) and after the All-Ireland we went to New York together when the team travelled to play Cavan in Downing Stadium. A few weeks later, Tom's wife, Toni, died of cancer. She hadn't been well on the trip to New York. I remember one evening in a hospitality tent lending her my tracksuit top because she was cold and miserable.

Toni's death hit Tom very hard. He didn't continue with Kerry, and in fact as a selection team we all pulled the plug around the same time. I struck out on my own with the county Under-21 team.

Tom remained a good friend and he's a good man to talk to at a time like this. Outside, in the county at large, the flaws in our team are being put under magnifying glasses so powerful that the whole of Gaelic football in Kerry seems on the verge of collapse. Tom sees the positive side of things as well, where we might be short a player or two, what might be done to work around the shortage.

By the end of the week I had my head well around it. Where we went wrong. What needs to be done.

★

At the end of my week in Kenmare I have almost gone through my grieving for a lost All-Ireland. I'm ready to move on. We have a meeting on Saturday night, Johnny, Ger, Pat and myself. We go for a walk down the demesne in Killarney and back up to Johnny's house, where his wife, Joan, makes tea and scones for us as always.

We establish the rules at the start. We've lost an All-Ireland so there's no holds barred at this meeting. We'll stay here till we find out what we did wrong and what are we going to do about it. It's the one time in our period together that we get cranky with each other. There's a bit of bloodletting in it. The sort of frank meeting you can have only if there's confidence that the friendships will survive.

I'm annoyed about a comment that appeared in the paper before the final about our star forward, Colm 'The Gooch' Cooper, needing protecting. It was some reporter who popped an innocuous enough question if you didn't think about the consequences. Is the Gooch going to be protected?

Of course he is, we would hope so. But the headline read like a call by Kerry for Gooch to be given special protection. I knew this was bad stuff as soon as I saw it. It gave the impression that we were pleading a special case and putting pressure on the referee. That's the last thing we need. Earlier in the year when we beat Limerick, their manager Liam Kearns stated that Gooch had engineered the sending-off of one of their players. Limerick had used four different players marking Gooch at times and the rotation meant that each fresh marker could take his treatment of Gooch to the legal limit. In the end Mark O'Riordan went over the line and got the red card. I felt that Kearns's words were hanging in the air all summer for referees to discuss. The last damn thing we needed was for the Kerry camp to be looking for special protection for the Gooch, going into an All-Ireland.

And what happened? Any ref looking at that will say to himself that Kerry can forget it if they think I'll be treating this Gooch fella with kid gloves. An innocent comment, and that's the way it works. It gets twisted around. As Mr Pacino says, it's a game of inches.

We lost an inch. After a good start Gooch got hit with a flake at a time when he was threatening to cut loose. It affected Gooch for fifteen minutes before half-time. He was out of it for a while.

Now, there were two umpires looking at this. The referee came in and warned Colm Cooper not to retaliate. You don't tell the player not to retaliate if nothing has happened. That aspect was disappointing. The crowd behind the goal was baying for blood, they had seen what had happened.

Gooch came to. Just before half-time he planted his feet in front of Ryan McMenamin to win a ball and the ref gave a free out. He was standing something like sixty yards away. The free was for what? Nobody had any idea. The ball went downfield and ended up in our net. I still talk to Gooch about that incident. If you know him, you'd know it was a six-point turnaround. If you know him, you know the way he plants himself. He was in a position in the middle of the goal and he was thinking *goal*. He says it himself. He had the net in mind with that one.

And in the final minute of the game (which was a minute shorter than it was supposed to be anyway) Peter Canavan's last act on the big stage was to cynically take the Gooch out of it. Gooch gave off a pass, went for a return and Canavan just took him and flung him to the ground. Probably nobody knew better than Canavan how badly unprotected a star forward can be in this game. He knew too that no referee was going to send Peter the Great off in his hour of glory. He knew what had been done to him by so many other teams (Meath in 1996 is one I remember well). So we suffered. Maybe it didn't change the match, but small things like that add up. Inches.

I had always said to our players that if there was an incident they were to stay out of it and let the linesman or the ref deal with it. I decided after that never to tell a team to go out on a field and stay out of it. As I see it now, when Gooch got that first smack, if a couple of our players had gone in that day and got a hold of the culprit, the referee would have been forced to do something. Our fellas, and this was my fault, stayed out to let the officials deal with it. I tell the lads again and again, we have to be paranoid. The bastards *are* out to do us. By any stretch of the imagination, I don't care what anyone says, Gooch was hard done by.

A part of me feels that Tyrone were fated to win anyway. How could we get players to go to the limit when we've won an All-Ireland semi-final by thirteen points? If I had my time again I'd push them to the edge, I'd drop a fella, a high-profile player, just to cause a ruction, a bit of rumpus to get them going. We were in the comfort zone and that's one bad place to be.

Again and again in Johnny Culloty's house I make the argument for tackling. Others make the argument for more toughness with the players. We want to create an edge. Without noticing it, we have gone from talking about the season just passed to talking about the season ahead. Whatever chance there was of us stepping down and walking away has gone. We decide in the end that we can't leave it like this.

After that meeting I've got a list put together for myself. First thing is to organize a meal for management and wives for next Friday. We'll need to mend a few fences after a raw, hard meeting and a bit of bloodletting.

The rest of the list is simple things. To be my own man. To be a little more ruthless. I think, looking back, there were a couple of fellas whose form maybe wasn't great. I've decided that we'll be picking players on training ground form from now on. Nothing else. One more year. We've won an All-Ireland and lost one. This coming year will decide how we're remembered. If we go down, it'll be on our own terms and it will be with everyone singing from our hymn sheet.

And funny, I can't but help thinking of my mother again.

I was my mother's pet. I was the youngest of a big tribe and I was a small bit spoiled. In the family it would have been known that I was her favourite. Even when she was dying in the hospital I'd have been fierce close to her. She wouldn't call me Jack at all, she thought Jack was too common a name for me. There was three or four people only who called me Jack when I was growing up. My brothers, mainly. They called me Jack after our Uncle Jack in

New York. My mother would remind people that I had been christened John.

My sisters and my mother would never even utter the name Jack, and Bríd Langford, my English teacher in school, refused to use it either. She thought it was common, like Shakespeare's Jack Falstaff.

So my mother called me John or Johneen. When she'd put the 'een' on to something, it was a term of endearment. She was in hospital, dying, when I got close to becoming the Kerry manager. Her last words to me were, 'Johneen, *a chroí* don't take that job at all, they'll be giving out to you.'

At the time I was sitting beside her bed in a hospital ward with a copy of the *Sunday World* rolled up on my lap. In the *Sunday World* was an article by Pat Spillane, an absolute royal among Kerry footballers with his eight All-Ireland medals. He was talking about his friend Páidí Ó Sé, another blueblood brother with eight All-Ireland medals of his own.

Pat said that things were at a poor pass in Kerry when the county board were replacing a legend like Páidí with a fella whose last entry on his CV was being beaten by Waterford in the Under-21 championship. Not a single reference from Pat to any other achievement in Kerry football which might qualify me to manage the county.

I haven't even got the job and I'm reading that. I'm alone in the ward with my mother as she's dying. I'm fine with Pat now, we've had it out, but those words stuck in my craw at the time.

'Johneen *a chroí*, don't take that job at all, they'll be giving out to you.'

I got the job and took it and told myself that Mother would help me more from the other world than from this one. A series of bluebloods had managed Kerry since their own golden days had ended, and now a *cabóg* from Dromid was in charge. The 'giving out' was about to begin.

2

Looking back on 2005, there's a few things I shouldn't have done. I ran for half the season on an empty tank. The flatness I was feeling spread to the players.

We'd flown through the 2004 championship, ending up with an All-Ireland to add to the league we'd won before the summer. The season stopped but I didn't. I was on a high. The dial in the brain was still switched to football twenty-four hours a day, but the football was gone.

So I got involved, helping out with South Kerry and with Dromid in their championships. Those campaigns gave me my fix right up until Christmas. The adrenalin never stopped pumping.

I was mad for action. One weekend I went over to London to a 'Kerry Person of the Year' awards shindig being held on a Saturday night. Danny Tim O'Sullivan, a great Kerryman, was being honoured over there. I never went to bed on the Saturday, I left the function and got a spin straight to the airport. We got back to Kerry and I drove Bridie down to our home in St Finan's Bay, had a quick bite to eat, togged off and headed straight to Tralee for the county semi-final, South Kerry against St Kieran's.

There must have been a desperate *cruth* on me. I must have looked the worse for wear. South Kerry got home by a point, and Laune Rangers accounted for Gaeltacht fairly handily in the other game. My involvement wasn't huge, but I'd got involved and I was living every kick.

The end of the year was as hectic as anything that had gone before. South Kerry won the county championship and then on 18 December Dromid won the South Kerry title for the very first time. The next week is a bit of a blur.

After Christmas the Kerry team and assorted hangers-on went on holiday to Las Vegas and Cancún. It sounds good but it turned out to be a tough trip and, when we came back, reality hit me like a sledgehammer. I found the early part of the year such a struggle all of a sudden. I remember in 2004 an incident where John Crowley took the hump and I drove all the way to Ballincollig in Cork to talk to him, one evening after school. Thought nothing of it. Now I was finding it hard to get the energy to go to training. The bit of enthusiasm I could muster was all for me, there was none left to transmit to the lads.

One day I went to our local GP, Derry Gibson, and spent an hour and a half with him. 'I've no energy, I've no enthusiasm, I'm lethargic. Cure me, Derry.'

He went through my schedule. Wrote a lot of things down, looked up and said, 'Jack, you're completely burned out.'

This was late February, early March, and I was shagged.

Pat Flanagan had warned me that I was going to hit a wall. I'd be out on my walks at night in the weeks and months after the All-Ireland win, and I'd be ringing Pat or one of the selectors, talking about it all, going through it all kick by kick. Pat warned me a few times to come off the roller coaster before I fell off. I was on a total high, though, king of the world, and bulletproof too.

And by spring I was dead. The summer of 2005 was a long struggle for energy and excitement. We tried everything to kick-start ourselves, to force some bonding into the team, to make ourselves feel what we had felt in 2004 when we were looking to prove something to a Kerry public that had written the team off in the previous couple of years. There was an edgy sort of energy within the panel that got us through everything in 2004. A year later, we were plump and satisfied with ourselves. Tyrone saw us coming.

This year is different. When I signed on for this gig, it was for the standard GAA mileage rate and nothing else. That has always been the tradition in Kerry. Managers don't get paid. I drove to Killarney two evenings a week, three evenings a week, four evenings a week, whatever was required. I came home late. I slept. I did it all again.

This year for my sanity and for the team and for the family I have renegotiated.

I am a teacher in Cahirciveen. This year I work half days in the school. In the mornings I spread as much enlightenment as the curriculum allows. The lunch bell rings and then I'm a football manager in the afternoons. The county board reimburses me for the financial losses incurred by the arrangement.

In fairness I haven't had to battle for this deal. I said to the county board that for me this was the only way to operate. It was done. I used to go to training tired and cranky. I came home worse. The family suffered. The job suffered. The team suffered. It was craziness and it nearly cracked me.

With the job-sharing I am able to go home from school and go to bed if I need a rest. I get up and walk and straighten my head before training or whatever needs to be done. I have energy. I am able to talk to fellas without being on edge. If there's a problem in training this year, it won't be with me. Previously I wasn't doing the job as well as I should. I was burning it at both ends.

I'm addicted to exercise. It's my drug. In the afternoons I can get a fix which clears the head. So far I've trained, walked, cycled, run and swum. I have my best ideas in solitude. I'll hike up a mountain, solve every problem I can think of and come down and start ringing fellas. I have a routine for ringing fellas on different days. Any fella who has got a grievance moves up the rota till we solve the problem. Constant contact is important.

Still, with the league a while away yet, it feels like a huge commitment to us all to come back for another long season. I've sat down at home and talked seriously with Bridie. When my adrenalin is pumping and my head is in football she runs the family. The decision on another season had to be hers as much as mine.

I said to her straight: 'If you don't want me to do it, I won't do it.' It takes a great woman to put up with an inter-county manager. A lot of the time you just go home to sleep, and then you're gone again. You're agitated and cranky and neglecting things. You're only half a presence in the house.

You're annoyed half the time, and then you're going off for the walks in the wilderness to try to get your head straight. It's not easy for anyone to live with. Bridie is very supportive, though. I think she likes the *craic* and the buzz as well.

It's the endings that are hard. The season finishes so suddenly, but the head keeps going. I can't sleep well for nights after games. I lie there with my head still in the world of football and Bridie gets shut out.

It's not just me at the crossroads, either. I'm the lucky one who has been able to switch to a job-share arrangement. Johnny has a troublesome knee. He's saying he has to get it done early in the New Year and he'll be out for a couple of games. Johnny isn't a man to go at something like that half-crocked. If he couldn't give it everything he wouldn't be inclined to go at it at all, but I'm saying to him that Johnny Culloty at 50 per cent is as much use to me as any other fella at 100 per cent.

Pat has a young family, and the demands on his time are immense. I've known Pat for quite a while. He's a former sprinter, and his knowledge of training techniques and his ability to apply them and adapt them have been central to us.

He's a sensitive man and when we row he gets bruised, but I love it when we go to a big game and Pat takes a look at the opposition. He has this thing about legs and the legs of players who do endless laps in training. He can see the muscle wastage as they stand for the anthem or walk in the parade.

'We'll hammer these today, Jack,' he'll say. 'They've too much running done. Look at their little legs.'

And Ger O'Keeffe is one of the busiest men I know. Ger is a funny guy. The strange thing is, when we were putting together a team of selectors, I didn't meet a man or woman in the county who thought he was a good appointment. Ger is abrasive when he needs to be and he would have rattled a few cages in his time. From the golden team of the seventies and eighties he'd be one of the mavericks. I appreciate him coming on board because most of that gang wouldn't have touched the job with a long bargepole.

Ger is a structural engineer. His job is checking things out after they've been built, and as such he has to rub a lot of fellas the wrong way. That makes him a good selector. He's his own man and doesn't give a damn. If Johnny gives me the odd clip on the ear, I give the odd one to Ger and he always comes roaring back. What a man. I need him for his enthusiasm, his knowledge of the players and his ability to pick up the vibes and mood from the players. He doesn't have to pick their brains, he can just read them.

Ger will tell me straight even if I don't want to hear it. 'The meetings are too long . . . The players are bored . . . They're sick of the video analysis . . . You need somebody with that talent.' Ger is the one always looking for the best for the players. He's the one who does the thinking outside the box and the long-term planning. He can think six months down the line about the way we should be planning things. He has that sort of intelligence. I'm emotionally intelligent. Intuitive maybe. One on one, I have decent instinct, but I wouldn't have a quarter of Ger's academic intelligence and ability to organize. A mighty man.

The key to it all is the friendship we have struck up, the sense of us being in it together and not wanting to go on without each other. I'd find it hard to go out and have the same rapport with another gang.

As a group we've been through a lot. That applies to Johnny and myself especially, I suppose. In football he has been a father figure to me, a living connection back to the days of the great Kerry coach, Dr Eamon O'Sullivan. Johnny puts manners on me.

There was a league game up in Mullingar in 2004 and I was wired to the moon because we were playing Páidí Ó Sé's new gang. I was trying to make my mark and Páidí was trying to make his mark and there was no quarter to be asked or given. It was a bad, stormy day and we had big Mike Quirke inside at full forward and we were playing with the wind. The instructions were simple. Go the *módh díreach*. Pump it in to him. And it was working. We'd got two goals off it. Quirke made them both.

Then we won a free kick, about fifty yards out from goal. I'm thinking to myself that if we keep going like this we'll make hay when one of the boys taps the free out sideways. Immediately I went half mental on the sideline and drew a kick at a water bottle. Johnny wasn't long telling me to sit down there on the seat.

'There's Kerry supporters in behind you, watching you. They don't need to see that. Behave yourself, Jack.'

And like a schoolboy I came over and sat down on the bench with my head bowed till I got a bit of *misneach* into me again. He has that effect on me. When Johnny tells me do something, I do it. A man with fifty years of experience in Kerry senior football tells you something, you listen.

I could never take exception to anything he would say. This is a man with no ego. If he wasn't involved in the team he'd be up in the stadium in Killarney watching them train every evening anyway. After every All-Ireland he played in, win or lose, Johnny would go off alone, fishing, for the week. Away off out with him early morning on the lake. It would be dark when he'd come back in. By the time the week was over, everything had died down. He looked for the solitude. I've learned that from him, too.

I remember another day, a few years ago, when Johnny was involved in the Kerry Under-21s with me. One day at half-time in a game, I was leaving a few curses out of me to get a bit of steam into the lads for the second half. I got a call that evening. 'Tone down your language there. This is Kerry football, Jack.'

A week after our bruising meeting in Johnny's house, we all meet in Nick's of Killorglin with the wives in tow. We're not so serious or intense when the women are there to laugh at us. The meal reminds us of the friendship, and by the time it's done we're good to go for another season.

The next day we go to watch West Kerry v. South Kerry in the county championship.

Rough meeting too with Sean Walsh, the chairman of the county board, regarding a team holiday. Sean is a good man, but himself and myself serve different constituencies. I have to think of the players first. Sean has to think of them, but he has to think of the county board and the sponsors and all the guys who do bits and pieces around the place. I don't envy him having to deal with a truculent bollox like me.

The meeting deteriorates quickly. I'm suggesting a few days away with the lads (and just the lads, no hangers-on) and to give the players vouchers for a holiday which they can take later in the year at their leisure. Sean knows that the men in blazers who go to meetings all year want to go on a big team holiday. It makes them feel good, and they can bring the spouses too. Sean has to keep things sweet.

There's a proposal on the table for a team holiday to Barbados. The usual planeload. It involves coming back from Barbados on 13 January and spending seven and a half hours in London waiting for a flight to Cork, which adds up on the return to twenty-four hours of solid travelling. No thanks.

Last year's trip to Las Vegas and Cancún was an endurance test. There were so many people on the junket that the players felt overwhelmed and paranoid that they were being watched all the time. Pat Flanagan joined us a few days late and almost finished up in jail in Miami because the name of another Pat Flanagan, a terrorist suspect, came up on some computer file at the airport. He was held for ten hours. And even poor Sean Walsh, Mr Blueskies himself, spent a month in hospital when we got home, having picked up some sort of bug along the way.

There was no bonding and not a lot of fun. I want to do it differently this year: a short trip to New York, just for the team; a training week in Portugal; and a voucher for each member of the team towards a holiday after the season. We'll see.

We train in Castleisland in the weeks before Christmas. There's a running track there, and a bit of a pitch in the middle, where we can play some ball. It's for the routine, really. Just a matter of ticking over. A lot of the more established players aren't even here. We've said that for them it's discretionary.

The Ó Sé brothers, the likes of Tom O'Sullivan, Michael McCarthy, etc. – they show up the odd night. Pat Flanagan is doing some new stuff with weights upstairs and he calls the fellas in occasionally to show them the ropes. Other than that we work away with the hopefuls.

It's in our heads that if we are going to get some traction this year, we are going to have to get some new faces. It's easier said than done. Despite what we in Kerry like to think, we're not teeming with talent right now. There isn't a whole generation of great players being locked out of the county team by what we have.

One evening I get stuck in to a kid called Kieran Donaghy. He's a big, loping and likeable kid who's been hanging around the panel for some time now. I'm waiting for him to show me some bit of drive.

'Kieran,' I say to him, 'you're fucking around in this panel for two years, getting bits and pieces. You're half this and half the other. What are you going to do about it?'

He's nodding. Donaghy always seems eager when you talk to him. He plays basketball too and he's been on television a lot on a reality TV programme for aspiring footballers. They call him Star. He's eager about everything.

'Listen, you'll make it or you won't make it, but you can't keep messing around playing basketball and being Jack the Lad around Tralee. Half being here or half being there. Go into the gym. Put some meat on the bones. Do Pat's programme three times a week through to early spring. Grow some muscle. Cut loose at the football and I'll give you a cut at it.'

He nods eagerly again. I don't know what to make of him.

Pat tells me later that he's brought Donaghy into the Institute in Tralee a few times to show him the ropes in a gym. He's also got him use of the gym at the Brandon Hotel.

Apart from the odd little pinch at a fella like Donaghy, collective training is unsatisfying at this time of year. There's a need to let the lads away to do their weights, a need to set them free for a while, but there's no edge to anything we do in Castleisland. We're just trying to tip over, to stay in some sort of shape and to make a decent show in the league.

I say nothing at the sessions. When I came into the job first,

I barely said a word to a player for the first five weeks. It wasn't planned like that but there just wasn't anything of substance to talk about. You need a context. There's no point talking to players in a vacuum. When there are no games on the horizon there's no edge to anything a manager might be saying. It's hard enough to engage players' brains when you've something important to tell them. You try to avoid using your voice just for the sake of it.

I'm thinking about how different and how very intense the football sessions will be in 2006. Defend without fouling. Stay on your feet without fouling. Break tackles.

I plunder the Ulster GAA council website, which is full of essays and drills on tackling. I go and speak to people about tackling. I phone contacts in Ulster. What do Armagh do? What do Tyrone do? This is almost a betrayal of my Kerry blood, to be asking how they do things up north.

One day I travel to the Crowne Plaza Hotel in Dublin and meet with a very prominent northern football man who knows exactly what they do. (He has to remain nameless.) We sit for a few hours as he shows me drills, gives me ideas, opens up a new world of work to me.

If you can lose an All-Ireland final on turnover ball, as we did last year, it makes sense to work as tightly as Tyrone and Armagh do on tackling and dealing with being tackled. In Kerry we do drills to work on our catching and kicking and positional play, but I come away from the Crowne Plaza with a sheaf full of drills and ideas for teaching players how to delay and dispossess an opponent, how to work the ball through a series of hefty tackles in a confined space. Conditioned games. Competitive drills. A new level of physicality. We've been too soft on each other in training. We haven't prepared ourselves for the combat zone that the new football has created.

3

Toorsaleen is a hard, bleak bastard of a place. Ridges, hollows and grey rock. People who wear their lives on their faces. Dark mists hide the tops of the mountains and the lakes are black in winter. The stark beauty of my home place is in the names given to every spot. Coomliath – Grey Valley. Cnoc Rua – Red Hill. Cumar Dubh – Black Ravine. Talamh a bhric – Badgers' Home. Tooreenaerach – Windy mountain. Cloch Ramhar – The Fat Rock.

I was born the youngest of nine. Four brothers and four sisters. At one time my mother had five children under the age of three and seven of us under the age of five, including two sets of twins. And nothing in sight but rock and scutch and sheep.

We all grew up in a long, plain, whitewashed house with stone walls as thick as a child's arm, a rough yard around it, a hayshed and a turf shed added on. A yard for shearing sheep and a cow shed for the nine or ten cows that Father kept. We were reared with the smell of the sheds twenty yards from the house.

Sheep were the big thing. Shearing the sheep and branding the lambs. Our brand was TCT – Tadhg Connor Toorsaleen. My father's father. I can still smell the burning of that brand as the letters burned into the horns. The branding would take place inside and you'd make up this big brazier with coals in it until it was white hot. It was just a beautiful smell when you'd burn those letters into the horns.

My family has lived here a long time, planting spuds between the rocks, letting hardy sheep scavenge what grass they could. Men and hardy trees facing into the wind and the rain, and the fierce loneliness of the place.

My father had a couple hundred acres of useless slough and hill and a few fields below to save a little hay in. Just hard mountain, dotted with his couple of hundred sheep. We saved hay and turf, killed our sheep and pigs and a cow now and again. We'd salt the meat and sometimes there'd be a pig hung and splayed at the doorway just beside where we children went up the stairs for bed. It was frightening to catch that dead eye watching you as you went upstairs to your sleep but Father used to tell us we weren't to be frightened. He'd say none of us were scared when we saw any part of a pig lying on a plate. We weren't.

The mountain didn't give much back, but there'd have been no living at all to be made on Toorsaleen if it weren't for events that happened back when my father was a child. My father's Uncle Johnny left here, like many before and since, and he headed to America. He was a hard man and he ended up mining for gold in Montana, working with every nationality under the sun, desperadoes trying their luck.

Uncle Johnny was playing cards one night and won a lot of money, and when the money was won he stood up from the table went back to his lodging, packed his bag and left town before it was light. He'd won more money than anyone at the table could afford to lose. If he stayed, he'd have been murdered.

He kept moving, and wound up for a couple of years mining for gold in Alaska. He kept his money secret and hidden. Even when he came home, nobody, not even his wife, ever knew how much he had come home with.

Around here we seem to be short on surnames. Most people are known by a nickname connected to the place they live in or some distinct characteristic. My great-grandfather had a touch of the old facial hair and he was known as Mickey na Whiskers. The rest of his tribe were just known as na Whiskers. I'd be Jack Whiskers.

Our neighbours on the mountains were known as the Mickey Mórs. We had a small parcel of land and the Mickey Mórs rented a farm from people called the Coyners. The Mickey Mórs were dairy men who rented the land and looked after the animals for the Coyners. The word was that the Mickey Mórs didn't take great care of business, they'd have the sheep down in the field and the cows up in the slough. The Coyners were fed up with them. The farm was to be sold.

As things stood, the mountain opposite was commonage. There was a boundary fence up by a spring well and what was beyond that was treated as common grazing land. If it went under the hammer, that would change. We Whiskers would be starved out of it. Uncle Johnny advised the family to buy the land.

This had to be done without the Mickey Mórs finding out who was buying it. My family must have known that the Mickey Mórs had money or were being backed by money. If they caught wind of who exactly was bidding for the land, the price would be pushed up and up.

The auction was held on the street in Cahirciveen, outside the courthouse. Uncle Johnny got a man called Tim Cronin, a cattle buyer from Milltown, to do the bidding. They bought the mountain and all the struggle and heartache that would come with it. It cost £750. That was in 1926 and my father was seven or eight years old. Back then, £750 was a fair, tidy sum of money for good land, never mind what Uncle Johnny had bought for the family to survive on.

Through Uncle Johnny's adventures in America the family had the money, though. The Mickey Mórs were left with a bellyful of bad blood towards us but nothing else. Sometimes survival is about spite.

Johnny had to be repaid, of course. The new farm had slowly to be stocked with animals first, however. My grandfather had no money to buy stock in 1926. He had a few sheep and a stony mountain. The sheep multiplied slowly, but if Johnny hadn't bought the mountain my grandfather would have had to leave Toorsaleen.

When my father got to the age of thirteen he was given, as he says himself, the present of a scythe and was put in the fields to start his slavery. By then there were some animals on the farm, and the family survived, selling butter and eggs in Cahirciveen. Chasing sheep, milking a few cows, making butter. A living.

The bargain with Uncle Johnny was that my father went across the mountain every September (the month for selling sheep, cattle and wool) to Johnny with £100 as part repayment. A few weeks of his labour would be the other part. Far from feeling important as he went, he knew what was before him: gathering hay, digging spuds. My father's brother Paddy went over to Johnny's house permanently when he was eight or nine years old.

It sounds a lot to say that any family had more than a few acres. For what it took to raise a family on Toorsaleen, though, people might have been better doing, as many did, closing the door of the homestead behind them and leaving the house to become a little *fothrach* between the scutch and the stones.

We lived most of our lives with no electricity, no running water and no car. We were lucky and happy to have a few old battered bikes about the place. Times were a little tough but we didn't feel too deprived. We never knew enough about what we were missing to feel that we were missing anything.

The loss of an animal haunted people. At one time there was a dog coming to the valley at night and killing sheep. My father sat up all night every night with a shotgun, trying to protect what he had, and his working day would start perhaps with the sight of another savaged sheep on the hill. Finally my brother Mike was taken from school to share the burden.

There were stories that were told often. The Murphys of Carrigina were wealthy ranching people. They would have had a couple of hundred of their cattle wandering the mountains at any time. Nobody else had grazing animals, so there were no fences and the Murphy cattle wandered where they might. Near Simléar Dubh (Black Chimney) one day, an animal went down. In other words, she broke the banks and went down over the cliff. The animal was roaring in fright and the rest of the herd ran towards her.

That image comes back into my head often when I stand, looking down at Coomasatharn Lake, all these huge dumb animals tumbling one after the other down the rocks to the cold black water, half a mile below. The sight of it and the tragedy for the man who owned them and his livelihood also gone down the mountain.

We suffered, too. Many years later, after my father was married, there was a coat of black frost for a few days which kept him off the mountain. When a thaw came, my father went out and missed seven or eight of his sheep straight away. When your life depends on animals you can tell if there's one missing just by looking at a flock. He went looking. He suspected they would be found on the cliffs. Sometimes the animals would scramble down the shale to little grass benches or shelves where they might feed. Then they'd be stuck there. He went down to Coomachoillean and there he found them. They'd gone down but wouldn't be coming back up. They were heaped, dead, all in the one spot.

For many people in Kerry and beyond, Sundays were for Gaelic football. They played it. They listened to Micheál Ó Hehir on the radio. In September they got the ghost train from Cahirciveen and went to Dublin to see Kerry in the All-Ireland.

My pastime on Sundays was going to the hill with my father, searching for our sheep. There was no fence and the animals, by accident or design, would go way down the cliffs on the other side. Father would go down after them. Down into Cumar Dubh. Up Drom Ruadh. Over Sagart.

On Sundays we'd go to Mass in Caslagh, in the building where I sat in primary school for the rest of the week. The first transport we got was a tractor. There'd be ten of us starting out, heading off down the hill, standing in the trailer as my father drove us down for Mass. We'd pick up neighbours along the way. There'd be bikes and God knows what else stuck in the back of the trailer and my grandmother would be in there, sitting on a chair in the middle of it all.

We were quite a sight, the mountain people coming down for Mass. I can remember going down one day with Grandmother sitting on the chair and Father took a turn sharpish and the chair tipped over. We had to let out a few roars to tell him to calm down.

For Father, pulling us along behind the grey Massey Ferguson was progress. When he was confirmed in the church at the age of twelve, he drove a horse and cart himself, with a dozen other young fellas in it, all down to be examined in the catechism by the priest and then to be confirmed. Every neighbour's child, and my father at twelve years of age driving the horse and cart through the mountains on the way to the confirmation ceremony. Not a parent in sight.

On the Sunday afternoons when I was young we went off to the mountain after dinner. Father would have the gun with him to shoot any foxes that would be after our lambs. We'd head off up Toorsaleen and beyond and not get back until dusk. It wasn't the most entertaining thing in the world but it was all we knew.

It was frightening too, sometimes, although maybe because I was the youngest I was spared the worst. Sometimes my father, myself or my brother Mike would spot a grassy bench down the cliff with a sheep stranded on it. We'd get to tying Mike on to the rope and lowering him down the cliff to rescue the sheep. Madness, but what were we to do?

Mike would be lowered down fifty, sixty, seventy feet of sheer cliff. Without a bit of *cur isteach* being put on her, the sheep would starve – and a dead sheep was no use to any man. Sometimes Mike would use his hands to dig out some sort of rough path for the sheep to come back up. At other times, when the drop was too sheer he'd have to be pulled up holding the sheep in his arms.

Mike had a passion for the work and he was fearless. At other times he'd go off on his own to save a sheep, his life depending on an old rope he'd tie to some rock. He'd do the work all by himself. If he could hunt the sheep back out of the bench, well and good. If he couldn't and the animal was too heavy for carrying, he'd tie the sheep's four feet together and risk his life doubly by climbing back up the cliff, this time without using the rope. Then Mike would pull the animal up.

When talking about somebody who has gone over the cliff to a bad end we'd say that they were 'clifted'. It was a hazard of life, being 'clifted'. There was a local sheep farmer, Michael Foley from Tooreenaerach, who got clifted and landed on one of the benches halfway down the fall. They reckon his dogs howled and sniffed for a few hours, looking for a way to him, before they headed home. Michael's brother Patrick found the dogs outside the house, crying. Patrick knew straight away what was wrong, but instead of following the dogs he went over the mountain to the Houlihans to ask for help.

Darkness fell. They couldn't start the search until first light. Next day they found Michael dead by the side of Coomasatharn. He'd had enough life in him to drag himself down to the edge of the lake. If Patrick had listened to the dogs, he might have found his brother in time.

One Sunday, when I was in my teens, we were high up the mountain when my father found a fox sleeping in the sun. For once he didn't have his gun with him and he sent me running down the mountain for it. I ran down, maybe two miles cross country. I ran back up.

While I was gone my father had been distracted by other work and had gone away somewhere. I decided I'd kill the fox myself. I lined up my sights with my hands shaking. This would be my first victim, but my mother would know that Johneen had killed the fox. It would be a proud day. I decided that I was a bit too far away from the sleeping fox to get a clean shot, so I started creeping a bit nearer.

Next thing I knew, I had kicked a stone. The little bastard woke up and he was gone before I could even raise the gun. The sense of disappointment and failure almost crushed me. It would have been like winning the sweepstakes if I'd shot the fox. I was about sixteen or seventeen then, and I knew I had screwed up. I still know it. When the story comes up even now, my father still can't laugh about it.

There's a black ledger which has been gathering dust on top of the dresser in my father's kitchen for many years. It records some of the big events in our lives. How much we got for certain animals, incidents of strange weather or sickness. There is a simple entry in the ledger which is marked 17 November 1976, a time when I was sixteen years old. 'We got the light today,' it says. The rural electrification scheme, which started in 1946, had finally found us in Toorsaleen thirty years later. We got the light and we left behind the candles and the old Tilly lamps with their kerosene perfume. According to the black book, we had got our first car just a few weeks earlier, and that Christmas we got a television. We watched John Wayne in *The Alamo*.

The world changed, but not too much. People still came to the house on bike and by foot. The people of my mother's age played a card game called thirty-one. You play with five cards, eight players a time. That was a social life.

The February after the light came, we got a fridge. Again the world stayed basically the same. No supermarket opened on the mountain. We still ate cured meat and plenty of spuds. Our own stuff. Everything by hand. Grown and pulled.

A big event for us was when Jimeen Curran, the butcher from Cahirciveen, would come out to the farm to haggle with Father for wethers (two-year-old sheep with their stones broken). We'd watch Curran through the windows in the yard with my father, the haggling going on for a whole morning sometimes. Curran turning to walk out the gate and down the hill. My father turning to come back in. The pair of them always going back and arguing some more until a spit on the palm of the hand and a shake on the deal. Sometime it might be a shilling they'd been arguing over, but it was a point of pride to try to get a better price from Curran than any of the neighbours got.

The good days were in the summer. Up in the slanted field, saving hay in the sun or footing turf on the bog. We liked the work, a big slew of us up there on the bog and my mother arriving up with big bottles of tea wrapped inside socks to keep them warm. Dark, stewed tea and heaps of sandwiches.

Sometimes we'd go to our mother's home place to help out. We'd cut brown bricks of turf with our Uncle Mike all day and draw it home a few weeks later with the donkey. Mike was a very positive man, always happy. Nothing ever got him down. We loved being around him.

My mother was from a few miles away in Glencar, so she was

well used to the hard ways of the world when she came to Toorsaleen. She grew up in a part of Glencar called Leitergorrive, or Rough Hill as it would be in English. No place was ever so well named. There's a joke about a Yank stopping the rental car in Glencar to admire the desolate scenery, and a skinny goat looking up at him and saying, 'Hey, the scenery is great but there's nothing to ate.' That's Glencar. Three miles of bog road got you to where my mother's people lived on the side of bare hill overlooking Cloon Lake. They grew some spuds and vegetables and fed a few sheep on what was left. They lived in the sort of place you could only be driven to by desperation or Cromwell, or both.

Mother had seven miles of a walk to school in Boheeshil and seven miles home again. You can't imagine a purer desolation. When she was sixteen she left for England and kept house for an executive of ICI. She lived for a couple of years there and then went to Boston to work.

At some stage she had met my father at a house dance in Mikey Gilpen's. From the road near Bealach Oisín you can still see the outline of the Gilpens' house, just a *fothrach* in the grass below. They had a courtship through letters, my grandmother sometimes writing on behalf of my father. Finally she came home and they were married and installed in Toorsaleen. She came with a dowry of £500, which went to my grandfather.

The family grew quickly, but before I arrived disaster struck. My brothers Paddy and Joe were playing with a box of matches one day and set fire to the hayshed. The flames swept through the barn quickly and caught the house next door. The fire burned away half the house. If you look at the roof even now you can see where half the building got taken away.

Only that neighbours saw smoke and came and hacked away a gap in the wall and roof at the halfway mark, the entire house would have gone. The gap acted as a firebreak and saved somewhere for us to live in. The whole thing gave my mother a bad fright. She had asthma anyway, and the trauma and the smoke she inhaled made things worse.

Mother had to go away from Toorsaleen for six months to the

Richmond Hospital in Dublin. The only time my father has ever been in Dublin (or outside Kerry) in his eighty-nine years was on a visit to see Mother in the hospital then.

As I say, I hadn't arrived yet. Caít, the sibling nearest in age above me, was still a baby. My Aunt Kate in Glencar had lost four children to cystic fibrosis. We gave my sister to her and Caít was reared there.

At the end of the day I don't know that Caít would have appreciated that. At the time there wasn't much choice in the matter. My mother was in hospital. The family were *trí na cheile*. My aunt longed for a baby.

Mother came home eventually. I arrived as an afterthought somewhere along the line.

The youngest. John. Johneen. Jack.

4

I'm an outsider. When you grow up on Toorsaleen you'll be an outsider everywhere you go except your own parlour.

In Kerry we make up for our remoteness from the world with our ability at football. It's a cliché but it's part of the identity of the county and its people, part of the way we express ourselves and project an image of Kerry for others and for ourselves. We win and we win with style. Our own style.

There's a type of footballer, the classic Kerry stylist, who we'll always elevate above all others. The Mick O'Connell or the Maurice Fitzgerald, the man who plays in the style we see ourselves as having invented. The pure footballer.

Within the divisions of the county, which are strong and distinct, I think that those of us living down here in South Kerry would see ourselves perhaps in the same way as Kerry sees itself in the bigger picture. We'd feel that we play the purest football, and that the way we play represents us and expresses us. We are outsiders, though. It's always said that a young fella from South Kerry would have to be twice as good as anyone else before they'd get a look-in on a county team. The townies have that scene sewn up.

And then cut the cake again. Within South Kerry, within our own little corner of the Kingdom, we would know that Waterville, with its more genteel, anglicized background and its easy way of winning local championships, would look down on us mountainy men from poor old Dromid, a place which never won a single championship before 2004. Dromid, whose little club was founded originally out of spite for Waterville.

Even within Dromid, our dark mountain of Toorsaleen wouldn't be football country. Here in the outsider county, we're the outsider's outsiders! I nourish myself on that. Sometimes I resent it but I wouldn't want to be anywhere else.

When I was involved training the schoolboys in the Kerry Techs, back in the early nineties, I'd say it to the Tralee and Killarney boys, winding them up. They had it handy, I'd say; back in Dromid we were the poor relations, the mountainy men, half savage.

I think, because of all that, I would always have felt a little bit of strain in my relationship with Mick O'Dwyer. He's a Waterville man, even though he played a year or so with Dromid when he was younger, and I played three years for Waterville myself when I fell out with Dromid.

A good part of those three years were spent training under him. I remember his enthusiasm mainly. Tactically he wouldn't have made things complicated for us. Getting the ball to his son Karl was our main ploy, as he was our best scorer.

I expected more from him when our paths crossed in later years. I remember going away up to Kildare once for a challenge game when Páidí was in charge and I was a selector. This was around 1997. We were in Newbridge, and Dwyer, who was a king there, came out to welcome Páidí, his prince. Dwyer greeted the other Kerry selectors warmly. He ignored me completely.

It didn't sit well with me. Perhaps it was to do with Karl. Maybe he thought that as the South Kerry man in the selection room I hadn't pressed Karl's case hard enough on the county team. Anyway, Karl made his own point. He transferred to Kildare and got himself an All-Star the following year.

I don't really care what Micko's reasons were for snubbing me. He was a neighbour and it shouldn't have happened. A few years later, when I got the Kerry job, I thought that Mick O'Dwyer, after all he'd won, could have given an old phone call, politely offered some advice over a cup of coffee. There was nothing. No goodwill. No word. Not one of the seventies team or the four-in-a-row men called up. There was just a silence for the poor rustic from Dromid as they waited for him to screw it up.

Perhaps I just wanted a bit of approval, some bit of a stamp or a brand that identified me as one of the herd, even though I was never a county man. I remember, on the day before the 2004 final, driving to Killarney to join the team for the trip to Dublin. I stopped off in Cahirciveen. In to Relish for the quick cup of coffee. Superstition perhaps. Hardly a day of life passes without me going in there. I took a quick, brave glance at the papers. Dwyer was writing a Saturday column at the time and it was his words I was looking for. Perhaps there'd be a benediction to send me on the way.

No such luck. Micko's thoughts were on the pandemonium that surrounded the dropping of Mike Frank Russell for the next day's game.

'He's just trying to get my pulse going, the old hoor,' I said to myself. I rolled on towards Killarney.

They work almost as a cartel, those boys. In Kerry it's as if they'd invented football and, for all they achieved, it's hard to begrudge that notion. They gave us great pleasure and eight All-Ireland titles in the golden years – but the game moved on. In Kerry we went from Dwyer to Mickey Ned O'Sullivan to Ogie Moran to Páidí Ó Sé, looking for a man who could make the world the way it had been again.

Then the Kerry county board came looking for me. And the silence from the lads was deafening.

An outsider? Sure. Sometimes it's hard to feel otherwise.

In January 2006 we went to the Gleneagle Hotel for the Kerry Sports Star awards. Myself and Bridie and my fellow mentors and their partners all sat together. Big night, big crowd. Micheál Ó Muircheartaigh was master of ceremonies and when the time came Micheál moved through the tables, squeezing comments from those who should have something to say.

My turn comes early. I supply the usual hopeful *raiméis* that managers spin out at the beginning of the year. The spotlight moved on and a few minutes later lit upon a table of golden-agers. Dwyer, Jimmy Deenihan, Bomber Liston and the boys.

At the time, it was being touted about the place that Jimmy Deenihan and Eoin Liston would be commuting to Laois as specialist coaches helping Micko. There was some excitement in Kerry about this. Maybe the boys were having a dry run for Micko and Bomber doing the Kerry job together next year. Anyway Ó Muircheartaigh slid over to Dwyer and asked him who would win the 2006 All-Ireland.

'Tyrone,' Dwyer said quickly.

The microphone moved on around the table. Jimmy Deenihan said some nice words about his old manager and concluded rousingly, 'We all hope that Micko will be brought back to finish out his great coaching career as manager of the Kerry team. We'd love him to finish up training Kerry.'

Applause. A few whoops.

I looked down at the plate and just wondered to myself: 'Jesus Christ. Am I only imagining it? Do I have this job at all?'

For the sake of the table I put a face on and said to myself, sure fuck them anyway, but I was mortified. Bridie sitting beside me, the selectors and their wives all around. I considered walking out of the function altogether, but that would bring more embarrassment and attention. I sat and thought about how it would be if I was whisked up to Laois for a similar dinner and somebody put the spotlight on me and said, 'Jack you'll have to come and train Laois after this year when we get rid of the loser we have doing the job.'

Afterwards Ger had a couple of words with Deenihan. Pat Flanagan spoke to Bomber. They told them it was outrageous. I doubt that the lads were worried. In their heads the Kerry team is still their plaything.

It works that way in Kerry. The four-in-a-row team hover over everything. They still write the history; for instance, I've read an article written by Páidí crying about how his selectors deserted him in 1997. I was one of those selectors. Myself and Seamus MacGearailt packed it in. I tend to do things in two-year bursts anyway, so I wanted to shoot off on my own with the Under-21s, whom I had trained for the previous two years. Tom O'Connor had to leave because of his wife Toni's illness. Bernie O'Callaghan, one man who would have undivided loyalty to Páidí, stayed.

Seamus and Páidí had gone into the job together as a joint management team, but by the second season, 1997, Seamus's role had been watered down so that he was essentially a selector. He felt maybe he wasn't getting the fair crack of the whip he had been promised. The first year, Páidí took the physical stuff and Seamus did the football with the team. By 1997, Páidí was doing the whole lot. Páidí had decided to take the football for the league. The team won the league so Páidí continued in that role. Seamus's role was watered down a bit every time you looked.

After the Munster final in 1996 I think Páidí himself would admit that he lost focus for a week. We paid the price in the semi-final. We had overlooked it, though, and stayed loyal to him: and in fairness he was a different man the next year. It was us, though, who had deserted Páidí in the end!

Oddly, the selectors that replaced us in 1998 and 1999 (Frank O'Leary, Sean Counihan, Paul Lucey) were gotten rid of quite quickly themselves. Kerry had scored 2–4 against Cork in the Munster final of 1999. Something had to change, and it was the selectors who were sacrificed. There was much talk (in one newspaper article especially) of Páidí looking around to the dugout for inspiration at a critical moment and finding none was forthcoming. It paved the way for another change of selectors.

Páidí screwed me in 1999, too, with the Under-21s. We won the All-Ireland semi-final with fifteen points to spare over Roscommon. Two weeks before the All-Ireland final, Páidí carried off my five senior players – Tom O'Sullivan, Mike McCarthy, Noel Kennelly, Tomás Ó Sé and Aodán MacGearailt – for a week's hard training with the seniors.

I went to the county chairman and told him I wanted our men for the final. Páidí got through to him too and said, he's not getting them. This was in May. The Kerry seniors preparing for a first round against Tipperary. Useless.

I had it out with the chairman. It shouldn't have been done.

I got the players back when we had finished our preparations for the final. They were no use to us. They'd lost focus. Their heads were gone. MacGearailt came back injured. Our free-taker for the final. We went into that match badly prepared mentally, and we lost to Westmeath.

I thought at the time that if we had won that Under-21 final I might have got the senior job in 2000. Losing it removed me as a threat. Páidí didn't spend all that time above in Kinsealy and learn nothing at Charlie Haughey's knee!

I decided after that that the seniors were the only show in town and threw my lot in with Páidí again in 2000. I watched my back as I went about my business this time.

There's times when I'm reminded that when push comes to shove there's the aristocracy from the seventies and the eighties and there's the peasants, and if I fail in two out of three years in the Kerry job it will tell people all they need to know about the peasantry.

I got a glimpse of what failure could be like very early on after I got the job.

Picture this scenario. One morning in Coláiste na Sceilge at the end of the long narrow town of Cahirciveen I'm teaching away, pushing back the frontiers of ignorance as best I can. Meanwhile Páidí Ó Sé, who brought me into the Kerry scene almost a decade ago, is about to hold a press conference in a room in the Gleneagle Hotel, away in Killarney.

Nobody in the Gleneagle knows for sure if Páidí is the Kerry manager or the former Kerry manager right now. He arrives with an entourage of lawyers and friends. At the same time I get a call in the classroom. The press conference has started. Come to the principal's office. A few minutes later, there I am inside the office, craned over a little transistor. It's like waiting for a war address from Churchill. Páidí might fight them on the beaches . . .

With me are the principal, Michael Donnelly, and Karl O'Connell, the vice-principal. We're glancing at each other at the end of every Páidí sentence. Is it yea or nay? Is he going to stay and fight the county board? Is he going to walk away? Only in Kerry could you have a scene like this, where the county stops to listen to a live broadcast of the senior football manager's press conference.

What the three of us in the room know is that I have been offered the job. I'm not sure if I was the first choice – the Waterford Under-21 defeat might have made me a hard sell – but I know that I have been tapped up. Maybe a few golden-agers have had their knees squeezed in the past few weeks.

The three of us in the office silently parse every word of Páidí's. The word is that the county board have given Páidí an ultimatum, to resign or be pushed. I've decided that if Páidí wants to stay and fight the board, that's his right. Seven or eight of the senior players have signed a petition backing Páidí. If Páidí decides to dig his heels in, things will get tough. I know for sure that I'll walk away from it and leave him to it. If not . . .

In the end, as we listen to the press conference it becomes clear that Páidí is waving the white flag. In the office we three look at each other. We smile, but we aren't sure what to say.

The night I was ratified as the new Kerry manager I was taken up with my mother's funeral arrangements. Páidí came down to the house a couple of nights later with a mutual friend of ours, Jerry Mahony. We'd had our rows, but that was the mark of Páidí.

We've talked occasionally since then, but it has cooled a bit. It was obvious that I had taken his gig, and it hurt him. There'd be the odd little cut at me in the columns he'd write for the paper, the odd piece of yearning for Kerry to be led to greater glory by a dream team of himself and Micko. Once he wrote a piece on how to beat Kerry, which I didn't think was a very clever or patriotic thing to do.

I can't ever say I dislike him, though. Sometimes he just enjoys a good line. I saw him on telly once, asked how the four-in-a-row team would fare against the current side. Páidí laughed and said the game would be over in fifteen minutes. It was a fair old insult, but only Páidí could get away with it.

Having Páidí there banging the drum and having his three nephews on the team has always kept the pressure up on me. The first year in the job I'd only to look at the face of the chairman Sean Walsh to see we were under pressure.

There were times when I'd see Sean coming into training – maybe we'd be playing the Under-21s in a practice game and not going well. Sean would look haunted. I remember a famous night above in the Radisson Hotel in Stillorgan before the All Ireland quarter-finals in my first year in charge. We were playing Dublin, and Westmeath, whom Páidí had run to on the rebound from Kerry, were playing Derry. We were going badly. We'd actually played the Under-21s the week before and they nearly beat us in Killarney. There was a real chance that we'd lose and Páidí's boys would win.

We did something half mad just to put an electric shock through the team. We dropped Willie Kirby from midfield and brought Paddy Kelly in. Just to stir things up. I told Sean what we'd done. I've never seen a man look under so much pressure. In Kerry he was facing the gallows. If Westmeath beat Derry and Dublin beat Kerry, that was the nightmare scenario there and the chairman gone. Me next.

We got through. Dara Ó Cinnéide stuck a goal after a rebound off the post and we got away with a win.

The first few months were like that. Putting out fires everywhere. We had gone to Lanzarote in the first week of January, to a nice spot called La Santa. Pat Flanagan had new training methods that he wanted to teach the lads, and everyone had to learn new things. Pat is a former sprinter. He took a look and decided that many of the players' running styles were faulty. Fellas coming down on the flat of their foot or their heel. The heel was acting as a breaker.

Anyway, we had a lad with us from Beaufort called Dan Doona. He was a fine talent, a minor the year before. He'd done something remarkable in Croke Park the previous summer: he'd kicked a sideline over the bar from each touchline. Wonderful skill. Dan was flying in La Santa and we saw him as one of our trump cards for the summer.

One night the boys were given shore leave to go out and cut loose. You have to allow one night for letting off steam in a week of hard work. They went to some nightclub, and Declan O'Sullivan was getting picked on by a local when Dan intervened on his behalf. There was some sort of fracas and Dan ended up taking a karate kick to his face.

I got a call in the middle of the night. Early the following morning the hospital told us that Dan's jaw was in smithereens.

So here I am, the new and unproved Kerry manager, having to ring Dan Doona's mother to say that her son who is away with the Kerry seniors is being flown home to Cork for an operation. His jaw will be wired and he'll be sucking through a straw and out of work for six weeks. That was a killer. And then when it was done I just had to wait for the media to start calling me.

The rumours got back quicker than Dan did. That was a sign of things to come. Journalists called me, wanting confirmation from the horse's mouth. I lied. I said it was a training-ground incident. No big deal. Just a collision.

When we got home, though, most of the same journalists rang me again and told me that they knew the story. So, I coerced them. 'You go with that story and you're history with us.'

It wasn't good. I could have done without that sort of thing before I had my feet under the table even.

The La Santa incident didn't help Dan's career. He got back later in the year, but everything had moved on. He never really got a chance to catch up on the fitness work. He's in Boston now, playing football, but he's a fiercely talented man who I'd love to see home and in a Kerry jersey. He could have played a big part in the green and gold if things had run for him. He had that sort of talent.

Then I lost my first competitive game. A National League game. To Longford. The longest journey of my life was coming home from Longford that night. I just remember driving back with Declan O'Sullivan in the car beside me and not a word said. We all stopped for food, in Patrick Sarsfield's in Limerick, I think, and I hoped the ground would swallow me before we got back to Kerry and to people who knew us.

To make matters worse, the week before the Longford game we had been hammered by Galway in a challenge game outside Sixmilebridge. Absolutely hammered. Two games in to managing Kerry and I was beginning to wonder if maybe I had it all wrong. Perhaps this was a job I just couldn't do.

In Longford I'd had an old black woolly hat on and it was stormy and I looked demented, this mad distraught look on my face. A caretaker in the school stuck this photo of me up on the noticeboard. He thought it was hilarious, and probably it was funny. But when I got a chance I took it down. Not on my own patch. I wasn't ready for a laugh yet. That was a rough week.

We beat Cork the next week. Dara Ó Cinnéide, in a decent gesture, took time out from training with the Gaeltacht to come and play for us that night. He was captain and felt he should. I was grateful. Paul Galvin had his first scrape that night against Cork. He got a clip on the ear off one of Cork's Nemo contingent and all hell broke loose. I didn't honestly care. It was a good night. The crowd rose and lifted us over the hurdle. Put an end to the toughest five or six days of my football life.

Some fella had told me that after the Longford game some supporters had shouted at one of the county development officers, Mike Larkin, that I was gone. It seemed believable at the time, I suppose. The only consolation was that the criticism wasn't too vicious. The doubters thought we were so bad they'd leave us to disintegrate of our own accord!

When we beat Dublin in Parnell Park in our third game, our first win up there in eighteen years, we celebrated like it was an All-Ireland final. I remember the chairman grabbing me and swinging me around. There was some amount of steam bursting out of the valves that evening. We were all under pressure, and now beating Cork and Dublin had lifted it. There was a little bit of road between ourselves and the Longford disaster.

Politically, within the team that was a huge boost for me. The Ó Sé boys were away on duty with the Gaeltacht club, having a run to the All-Ireland club final, and by the time they came back we had some traction. After beating Dublin we lost up in Tyrone (with half a team) in the last regular league game of the year, but we had already qualifed. We lost it by a point, 1–6 to 1–7, and I made an optimistic entry in my diary, that I could see something big happening. We had shown massive resilience and had come away feeling as if we'd won it.

So when the Ó Sé's came back, we'd taken half a team to Omagh and lost by just a point. We'd beaten Dublin. Beat Cork. Beat Páidí's lads in Westmeath. We were in a National League semi-final without the Gaeltacht boys or the Gooch. If I'd lost three or four games by then, that would have been it. Instead, we had some unity and some achievement under our belt.

I'd sensed back in January, on the La Santa trip, that the O Sé boys, Darragh in particular, were still hurting over Páidí's depart-ure. Comparing the way the uncle they had grown up idolizing did things with how I operated was never going to work out in my favour. The boys are strong, influential characters and I won-dered how the dressing room would hold together if they didn't buy in.

Darragh would have a bit of the rogue in him. You'd have to time your moments with Darragh. Tomás is different: what you see is what you get with Tomás. And Marc up to this last year would have lived in the shadow of the other two, but he's blos-somed. They are so close as a family that they come as a package deal. I knew they were hurting a bit when I came in, so I made certain to walk on eggshells around them.

Within the squad they'd be clannish. They'd be good buddies with Paul Galvin since he joined the panel, and with Eamon Fitzmaurice. Paul works in Cork and drives in with Tomás. Eamon Fitzmaurice would come in from Tralee sometimes with Darragh. That's a strong nucleus of personalities to have to cope with as a clique. It wasn't always easy.

The absence of the Gaeltacht boys early on meant that we had to go out and find a couple of new players. We came up with Aidan O'Mahony, Brendan Guiney and Paul Galvin, which wasn't too bad. There were signs of rebirth in Tommy Griffin and William Kirby. The absence of the Gaeltacht lads worked for us on the political level, too. By the time they came back at the end of the regular league campaign, the show was on the road.

If there was any lingering resentment or bad feelings about Páidí, their time away from the team defused things. When the lads came back into training sessions, we were on our way and the other lads were in a pattern of conformity. I was very fortunate that Seamus Moynihan had given me an endorsement of sorts in the effort he was putting in and the interest he was taking.

Seamus was a key voice in the dressing room, a great supporter of the younger players. We were going to need those younger players to stay on board and not become disillusioned. I remember talking to John O'Mahoney the night Galway beat us in that challenge, and he said to me, 'You won't have many of them fellas next August.' I was thinking, August?

As it turned out, we had most of them the following August.

What we found when we came in to the job was that the spirits of the players were down. There was no talk or banter in the dressing room. They'd had three years of getting slaps in the head and kicks in the *cojones*. They weren't popular with the Kerry public, and Páidí had hung on for a year too long in the job he loved.

Lifting them up could only be done in two ways. Trying something a little different, a little new energy, a different style of communication, new ideas. And, of course, winning. By the time we got to the league play-offs in 2004 we were doing those things.

That was then, this is now. The pressure is on again for 2006, and I'm thinking of Páidí again. Even as a golden-age superstar he was forced in a low moment to admit that the Kerry fan is one rough old animal. Hard to please and slow to praise.

It's all ahead of us again.

5

After the long negotiations with Sean Walsh we have forgotten about the idea of a giant holiday for the team and for half the county. Instead, we get four days in New York in January for the panel, just the players and the management. Good bonding. A few basketball games in Madison Square Garden. Nights out in Hogs and Heifers. Each of the lads has been given a voucher for a private holiday later. And at the moment we are in Portugal for a training week while the National League takes a three-week break.

We sussed out a place called Brown's Club, down here in Vilamoura on the Algarve. It's a fantastic facility that has been used by Premiership teams like Bolton, Fulham and Middlesbrough, and by international soccer squads like Russia and Nigeria before big tournaments.

Under the sun you can slow everything down. You're not standing around in the rain and wind, with fellas straining to hear what's being said and wondering when they can get away for the night. There's gyms, pools, tracks and wonderful pitches. The lads stay in chalets, hanging in each other's company for the week.

One of the first things we worked out when we sat down as a management team after losing the All-Ireland was the tackle. We don't want to play like Tyrone but we want to tackle like them. We said last autumn that we would work big-time on the tackle. Rather than just talk about it, we will actually work at perfecting it. With most inter-county teams the only time you'll hear tackling mentioned is when a manager screams in desperation at a corner back to get a tackle in.

So the work starts here. Pat Flanagan hasn't been able to come to Vilamoura, he's had to stay home with the family. Johnny couldn't come either, so myself and Ger O'Keeffe have worked on the drills. Now it's happening. Great weather. Great surface.

Great privacy. Massive intensity. We get the fellas in little rectangles, breaking tackles, trying to stop players. Stopping them legitimately, that is, no short cuts.

The lads are enjoying it, I think. They can see the point and we've got some variation into the training. The tackling problem wasn't a case of lacking power; it was technique. We have to get the concept right. You don't tackle with your hands any more. You tackle with your body. We've had that wrong for a long time. If you play against Tyrone or Armagh and you slap at them with your hand, they have the solution. They'll pull your hand in close to their bodies and go down. You go down on top of them, looking like you've pulled them down.

We've looked and learned at last. Tackle with the body. You stop the guy, then you go for the ball. This is where Tyrone in particular have had it over us. They stop you first. They put their body in the way to slow your momentum, and then they go after the ball. We were putting our hand out and they were bursting by us.

We work on the tackle every day. How to do it, and then how to cope with it. Again watch Tyrone. They'll go in to a tackle, and if for some reason they don't ride it they have the ball laid off to a man coming at speed on the shoulder. What we do when we play against them, on the other hand, is we run into their bodies, decide too late that we're in trouble and start looking for the pass. Tyrone hold your hands and arms when you try to release the ball. They are masters at it. So you spill the ball. Six out of seven points in the first half of the All-Ireland final from turnovers! I wake up sweating when I think of it.

We put down hours, working on special drills to keep the support player running off the shoulder for a man going in to face a tackle. That off-the-shoulder passing work has to be done on the training ground. It has to be automatic. So we do these drills that teach us how to come out against heat. Players take the ball at pace into the tackle, but they have an out. There's no more slow ball. It's a double advantage to keep the ball moving but to suck the opposition in to contact.

The drills in Vilamoura are intensive, and bursts of sixty seconds or two minutes leave guys needing recovery. After this week we should be able to see the benefits of the work. Even the forwards are tackling properly. If a fella gives away a cheap free, the others are looking at him and cursing him.

Johnny Culloty has an old mantra from the Dr Eamon O'Sullivan school of Kerry football. Fear Fatal Fouling. Tackle properly, in other words. He has another one. Close Continual Coverage Without Fouling. Johnny often points out that Dr Eamon's philosophy still applies in everything teams do today. If he was here in Vilamoura, he'd be smiling to himself.

The league is important to us this year. Getting a run through to the play-offs is what it is all about for us. After that we'll play the ball as it lies. Whatever comes along, we'll deal with it without trying to manipulate the situation.

We've had our first couple of games, and it's been a mixed bag: first, on a wet night in Tralee, we entertained our old friends from the west: Mayo 1–15, Kerry 1–14.

We conceded a goal in the first three minutes and for a lot of the game we just looked on as Mayo came running through us like a dose of salts. Mayo seem a bit too full of running for this time of the year, but we have a few problems of our own. Eamon Fitzmaurice got a lot of trouble from Ger Brady at centre back. We tried Tomás Ó Sé at midfield but it went badly. Tomás had to be taken out of there after twenty minutes and switched to wing-back.

There was no shape to us at all. At half-time we got the lads in and emphasized keeping the ball and working it in. We needed to be making their backs chase and defend rather than flaking the ball in on top of them. We talked about playing simple ball to our own half-forwards. We'd been chasing their half-backs up the field all day. The instruction now was to keep their half-backs honest. Engage them and let them work as as defenders.

It worked well enough, but we still lost.

We have a few positional troubles. We played in the McGrath Cup last month, and for the four games I had a distant relative of mine, Adrian O'Connor from Glencar, in at full-forward. Size-wise, Adrian is what we need. A big obelisk of a man, six foot five or so. When we got to the last game, against Cork, he bit off more than he could chew with Graham Canty. It's hard to find an obelisk with mobility.

Against Mayo we started with young Kieran Donaghy at wing-forward. There's a thought in our heads of trying him as a full-forward, but against Mayo we needed to move him back to midfield when Tomás switched. He did well there, and if he can get his temperament right he might be an asset this year.

In the McGrath Cup final, last month down in Páirc Uí Rinn, we took Donaghy off just after half-time and he shot away into the dressing room, and he was gone away off out the gate before we came in after the game. Tom O'Sullivan disappeared too. Tom is a rogue and I can live with that, but we didn't need young Donaghy aping him. Donaghy had to be hauled over the coals for that. It was my chance to give him a little slap on the wrist. We talked.

'Kieran, does this mean every time I take a fella off he's going to feck off down the town?'

Donaghy was apologetic and I was glad to have had the chance to make a point. I wasn't too bothered about what he'd done, really. Better for him to be pissed off about being substituted than not to care. Having a word with him let him know we are serious about him this season. It's all about context.

We're not sure how he'll work out for us. Donaghy sees himself primarily as a midfield player and he needs that ball work which you get in the middle. Full-forward is very specialized. Donaghy can do a few things at midfield and he can be the mobile one while Darragh anchors things. He has to establish himself on the team first, though.

Meanwhile we have work to do everywhere. Not just tackling. We need to develop structure at the back, to have solid midfielders and half-backs who'll stay back. Fellas tearing up the field, losing the ball and then haring back again is no good for us. Mayo gave us a lot to work on.

Our next game was against Cork. To beat them would be a fantastic boost before we came here to Portugal for the annual training week. To lose to them would be a disaster. That was enough motivation for this time of the year.

And beat them we did, with a five-point margin on a cold, wet night. Billy Morgan had a rant afterwards about us being the most cynical team in the country. The reporters came to me afterwards and told me that Billy was putting this line about. My jaw dropped. No idea where that is coming from, other than to think that the old fox is starting to lay down his markers for the summer already.

Against Cork, Darragh and Donaghy did well at midfield and Declan O'Sullivan won a lot of ball from Canty at full-forward. All good. It would have been hard to lift the lads if we had been beaten by that shower.

The Morgan stuff bothers me, though. Is he looking for a row or what is he at? I didn't react and I told everyone not to comment. The less talk there is about whether or not we are cynical, the better it will be.

Sean Walsh got asked about Morgan's words and couldn't help himself. 'No comment,' said Sean, 'but Kerry don't set out to play that kind of football.'

Jesus, Sean! That's a comment!

Here in Vilamoura, though, the atmosphere is good and positive. Most of the time. In the middle of the week the players are given a night out and the promise of no training the next day. It's a chance to get out together and relax and have a few beers and whatever.

Of course, lads being lads, there's the usual repercussions. A couple stretch it to a second night.

When we meet for the early-morning session on Thursday I do a head count. Two missing. I go half mental. Back in their chalet, Aidan O'Mahony and Mike McCarthy are just getting off to sleep.

I send John Joe Carroll, one of the county board boys, in to get them. No use. Mahony lets a roar at my man on the way out. 'By the way, John Joe, make sure you close the door gently after you on the way out!'

We do the morning session, anyway. At midday, when the sleepwalkers have returned to the fold, I bring it up. I'm going into a battle I know I'm going to win, so I'm confident. I talk about commitment. If they're not prepared to sacrifice a night on the drink we're going nowhere. Here we are in team meetings, talking about what we were going to do to Tyrone and Armagh, and we can't leave it be for a night.

Then of course I go too far. Aidan O'Mahony turns and storms off.

Yerra fuck it!

We do the training session. Somebody placates Aidan. High spirits again. It all works out.

6

When my time came, I did as my brothers and sisters had done and began walking the couple of miles down the road to Caslagh school, a tiny seat of learning near the crossroads. The girls had one half of the schoolyard. We boys had the other.

The headmaster, Padraig Breathnach, was old style. We lived in fear of him. Not speaking Irish was a mortal sin and got you punished with a stout stick. I remember the Maistír hit a young fella one day and the lad fell on the floor either through shock or unconsciousness. Padraig Breathnach didn't care either way. '*An bhfuil an diabhal marbh?*' he asked from the top of the room. Is the devil dead?

My brother Joe had a bit more bravery in him than the rest of us, and one day he got into a fight with Breathnach. I can't remember what was at the heart of it but I remember Joe, full of steam, running out the door, waving and shouting back, '*Slán! Slán!*' Our mouths were hanging open. Joe was like Cool Hand Luke, busting free.

Off home with Joe, of course, and up to Father saving hay in the field. He gave Father the breathless news of his escape. No sympathy there. Another clip on the ear and turned around to walk the couple of miles back down to school again with the tail between his legs.

We didn't live in a Gaeltacht in the strict sense of the world. Dromid is a *breac* Gaeltacht or semi-Gaeltacht area. There was some Irish spoken and the language runs through the place like a river with many tributaries. We use Irish phrases as if they were English. When we went to Caslagh, we had to speak Irish in school. There were a few clips on the ear from an tUasal Breathnach if we didn't.

The old football was the only entertainment. We caught bits

and pieces of Micheál Ó Hehir on the radio sometimes. I remember one match he was commentating on, Mick O'Connell and the boys off playing in the Cardinal Cushing Games from New York. He caught my imagination with that one, and for months afterwards I'd be walking along the fields, imagining I was the great Connell and commentating on my genius as I went. It was that which gave me the first spark of love for the game.

My father wasn't a football man and diversion wasn't high on the list of priorities in the house. We had some sort of a primitive old football all right. On Toorsaleen the problem was getting boots and finding a level bit of grass to kick ball on.

Most of my youth I played football barefooted. That sounds stark, but I wonder now, did I even think anything of it? I can't remember. We were all in the same boat, the brothers and I anyway. We'd run to the hill in our bare feet over stones and through rushes. Our feet were as hard as nails. It never seemed too odd to be playing football in your bare feet.

When I was thirteen or so, I got a hand-me-down pair of old Blackthorn boots that came up around the ankles and bit into them. They came down from my brother Paddy. I hobbled in them till they were broken in and then I hobbled some more. They weren't the sort of things you'd see Cristiano Ronaldo jinking around in.

My older brother Paddy was a good player. As a kid he was the business. He played Kerry minor for a couple of years in '73 and '74. He played with Páidí Ó Sé and a whole slew of fellas who would make names for themselves in the years after. It was Paddy, more than anyone, who instilled my *grá* for the football. He was a stylish, classy player, a good operator.

I was fourteen when he was playing minor and I could see the talent in him. He had a chance of making it as a senior, but he drifted a bit. He went into the Gardaí and they moved him around a bit. He married young and got responsibility early. For a while in the seventies he was a garda in Cabra in Dublin and played football for Oliver Plunketts along with the Brogan brothers.

As for our own club, the numbers were so small in Dromid

Pearses in the bad years that anyone who was fit and able played when asked. My eldest brother, Tim, played a bit, not too bad a player. Years after growing up, four of us played one day for Dromid in a match against Dr Crokes 'B' in Division Five. We played them up in Killarney. My brother Joe felt a bit left out, so he was allowed to act as a linesman. There was some bit of a rumpus in the second half and Joe arrived into the mêlée. He reckons the five of us were on the field together that day.

Paddy was the only star, though. We'd spend hours looking for good spots to kick football in. That was our obsession. There were old *gairdíns* with rushes and stones we could get some use out of. When the hay would be cut in the meadow we'd have plenty of room for a while. I hear myself talking sometimes now about the state of the surface in Croke Park or Fitzgerald Stadium and think back sometimes to the sloped little patches of green where Paddy and I kicked ball growing up, hoping not to go over on an ankle.

There were very few real matches to occupy your time. If you were playing minor you'd be lucky to have six or seven matches a year. There was no club in Dromid for most of our youth and we played minor with an amalgamated Waterville–Dromid team. Before that I can remember, at about fifteen years old, playing on an amalgamated team with Derrynane. They had a pitch of sorts up there. It had a forty-five degree slope on it and if you ran down the hill with your arms spread out wide your feet would carry you so fast that you felt like you were flying.

As minors we'd train in Waterville when it got serious, which wasn't for a very long period of any year. All the other kicking we'd do at home. Myself and Paddy would kick two hours every evening, seven evenings a week. Left foot and right foot. I developed plenty of skill and kicking ability, but I never had the athleticism to be a county player. I could pick a pass, though. All those hours in the field gave me plenty of practice at it. If I missed Paddy with a foot pass, the ball might bounce off down the hill. It was easier to learn to be accurate.

As I say, the club in Dromid just didn't exist for most of the time when I was growing up so, much as we liked football and the idea of it, the game itself was always a bit remote. When Dromid Pearses re-formed in 1976 after about twenty years of being obsolete, the club didn't exactly sweep the imagination of the whole area.

.The club had been founded originally in 1954 by a man called Sean Hard Curran, out of spite for Waterville, who had treated him poorly. Sean Hard drove the club for a few years until he was forced to emigrate to America in 1958.

(With typical Dromid spikiness Sean Hard made a point of playing illegally, and he could count twenty-three different clubs which he had lined out for before he retired. He'd played under almost as many different names.)

When Sean Hard went away to Chicago, football died out again and there was a little lull again till the mid-sixties. A few characters like Patsheen Connor and Paddy Casey and a few more got things going for a while in the old field, or John Mick's field as it was known. They took a lease from him and they played games there. No more than four or five games a year, travelling from one club to another. It wasn't uncommon to see men out playing for the club in their trousers. Some men had no knicks, and football wasn't big enough or frequent enough to bother buying a pair.

That revival lasted briefly and, when it died, Dromid Pearses didn't get started up again until the winter of 1976. A group of men met in the old school in Derrynane. Haulie Sé, who is now a successful developer of golf courses, proposed the colour of the jerseys the new club would wear. Other than that there was no field and no money. Just this notion that we in Dromid, as a small group of hardy souls sparsely populating a huge desolate chunk of the earth, needed a football team to make us into a community.

At about the time of the seventies revival there was a scheme introduced by the government to allow old farmers to retire and live off a pension. Jim White, a local farmer, was one of the first to take advantage of this. Jim took the deal, and the Land Commission said they'd let the club have a field of his. A Mr Temple gave Dromid Pearses a small field, maybe an acre in size, to train in.

There was some negotiation after that. A year or so later we got six and a quarter acres for £1,005. Dromid was a scattered, bleak place, still with no centre to it, but when the club was re-formed we had a team of our own at least.

What kept the club going at that time was travelling to festivals in the summer. There was a festival in Waterville, one in Valentia and one in Cahirciveen, and they each had Gaelic football tournaments. Dromid would go around, playing in seven-a-side competitions, hoping to get the whole two days out of the event.

Other than that, there were seven games to be had in the county league, four games in the South Kerry league and one (always one because we always lost it) in the novice championship.

At least we had a pitch and a team of our own. It gave us some sense of ourselves. At the time there was a bit of an affinity with Waterville, and fellas my age played for Waterville through the underage ranks. For instance Gerard Cronin from Waterville was a mentor to us from Under-12s to minor grade. We won out in all those grades on the way up. Gerard was our bus driver into the vocational school in Cahirciveen too. A good character and a Waterville man, but in some way we were always the outsiders, going down hoping for a game, looking to impress.

When I went to secondary school in Cahirciveen I played a bit inside in the school there. I remember getting on a Kerry Vocational Schools team in the late seventies and being delighted with myself. The great Donie O'Sullivan was our coach. Donie was good, good with players especially, and I learned a bit that year.

I'm not sure how it happened, but bad blood developed again between Dromid and Waterville somewhere along the line. The relationship changed when we began to take ourselves seriously, I suppose. It became a bit messy and it has stayed that way. All that unifies us is perhaps our sense of being from South Kerry and needing to prove ourselves doubly for the green and gold.

You never escape your home place. Especially if it's somewhere like Dromid that is in your blood. My best pal growing up was Sean O'Connor, or Sean Ó Coomlia as he is known, his family being from Coomlia. Sean and I would have been in class together in primary school and then in secondary in Cahirciveen. We're still involved with Dromid together, back where we both started. The place never lets go of you.

The first time I ever saw a Kerry team in the flesh was at a challenge game played against Tipperary in Cahirciveen. Mick O'Connell was the hero to every boy in South Kerry, this graceful legend who in the early years of his career rowed himself across from Valentia Island to Reenard to go training in Killarney on summer evenings. It was 1968 and I was seven, maybe eight years old. O'Connell was in his prime and I remember he became so uninterested in the game that when he got the ball a few times he kicked it up in the air and went leaping after it himself.

That was no fun if you were marking him and I remember later when O'Connell got old there were a few players about the place who took their revenge. For me, though, his athleticism and his style that day in the field in Cahirciveen were what football was all about. He really rifled the passes and he had that special style of kicking. He could throw the ball out with the right hand and kick it with the left, just send it spinning.

I never met Connell when I was a kid, but I observed him and studied him. I listened to Micheál Ó Hehir describe him, our man. He was a gazelle, the spring of him, straight up in the air.

In 1977 I saw him play in a South Kerry final. Waterville versus Valentia. I was playing minor with the Waterville–Dromid Combined Selection against Renard that day. I was at midfield and Neilie Cullen was in harness with me. It's so long ago that I'm teaching his kids now; poor Neilly died a couple of years ago of a heart attack. Anyway, we won by a couple of points, I was marking a Kerry minor, Frankie Donoghue from Renard, and I did all right.

When it was over, we boys watched the men coming out for the senior game. Connell was on a bit in age then, but he didn't come out the gate with the rest of them. He ran and jumped the wire. He had a pair of perfect white gloves on him at the start of a bad wet day, and he went sailing clear out over the wire in

Con Keating Park. We let a few yahoos out of us when we saw him leap.

The first time I'd seen him on television was back in 1968, the same year that I was brought to see him play in Cahirciveen. We had neighbours, the Sheehans, whose father was keen on the politics: he had nicknamed his two sons Cossie and Dev, for Cosgrave and de Valera.

Patrick Sheehan, who was known to us as Cossie, had an old, black, beat-up Volkswagen Beetle car, and he took myself and my eldest brother Tim into Cahirciveen to watch the 1968 All-Ireland final on television. Down beat Kerry by two points that day, but we drank our minerals slowly to make them last as we watched in Sheila Timothy's pub (or Sheila Connell's, to give the woman her proper name) in the upper east end of the town.

The television pictures were black and white, of course, but that was my first memory of the glamour of the green and gold in an All-Ireland final. My friend Johnny Culloty would have been playing that day also and, looking back, it was another of those sore defeats that Kerry have suffered to northern teams.

The first Munster final I went to was 1975. I think it was in Killarney. They cut loose that day in the green and gold and we came home, knowing it was the start of something. We still wouldn't have had the electricity at that stage and going to a Munster final was a big adventure. Otherwise it was television. There was a famous house five or six miles away from us – Jack Hallissey's. Jack had the first television in the whole of Dromid. We'd walk down there to watch the matches. I saw the 1970 World Cup on that television, and on Sunday evenings lots of the neighbours would gather there to watch RTÉ's famous old soap opera, *The Riordans*.

In September 1975 we watched the All-Ireland final in Jack Hallissey's – lads my brother Paddy had played with winning All-Ireland senior medals on the television. Anything seemed possible if you were a young fella in Kerry then.

The first time I was in Croke Park was for the 1978 All-Ireland final. We watched from the Hill on a bad day for the Dubs, watched Bomber Liston, the big man who was teaching down in Waterville, just cut loose in front of our eyes. Three goals in his first All-Ireland. It was a great period for us to be growing up. Massive success every year and games that set the pulses racing.

The most lasting images, though, are always of your first hero. I've become friendly with Connell over the past couple of years. He still has a great loose spring to him. An absolute athlete to this day. One of my proudest moments was meeting him on Valentia Island in 2004 after we had won the All-Ireland. We were touring the national schools with the Sam Maguire. He congratulated me on the style of football we had played. Coming from Mick O'Connell, that meant something.

7

In the winter you spend so long thinking about the season just gone by and so much time making fine plans for the year ahead that you forget sometimes what a season feels like. A season never turns on just one big idea. That's for the pundits. It's a thousand small adjustments as you go along. It's bad days and learning from them. It's a couple of hundred nights on training fields. It's reacting to a thousand and one things, and just stumbling on.

There's very little inspiration. Lots of perspiration. Lots of stress. It's not what you say at half-time. It's the work you've done for the previous month that wins the games. Small stuff. Not grand gestures.

And when the games start, they come at you like traffic. The league begins with a couple of matches and then it takes a three-week break, and suddenly it's rush hour. You're thinking on your feet all the time.

So, in our third league match of 2006 we beat Fermanagh by seven points. A good day. Fermanagh are no bad team and they made it hard for us. We've had a free weekend while they've been scheduled to play every week. They have beaten Dublin, Tyrone and Monaghan already. Things are working for us, though. We were a couple of points down, ten minutes into the second half. Declan O'Sullivan set up Eoin Brosnan for a great goal. It was nice to put one past their full-back, Barry Owens, who got Player of the Month for the previous month.

Seán O'Sullivan came on and scored two points for us. Seán will be an addition this year, even if only off the bench. There's worries, too. Mike Mac got taken for four points from play at the back.

Sometimes the things that turn a season are the things that nobody else sees. You go to a game in some godforsaken place on a miserable day, and you pull out a result that nobody else notices.

For us this year I think that day will be the league game against Monaghan in Scotstown. The game brought back memories. You get an instinct. I got a feeling, driving to the ground in the morning. Driving north on a dreary, miserable day. It was raining and when we got to Scotstown and looked at the place, I said to the lads that this was a cauldron. Eight thousand. Tight ground.

The local stewards made a rumpus about putting the selectors outside the wire. Johnny was getting fierce agitated, talking about rules, until they gave in.

Before, in the dressing room, I told the lads it reminded me of being up in Kingscourt in Cavan in February 1997. In 1997 on a bad wet day the ground in Kingscourt was heavy and we got out of there with a win. A couple of points after coming from behind. Cavan had sixteen wides. It turned our season. We believed after that one.

'This game is monumental, lads,' I said in the dressing room. 'If we get our arse out of here by one point, we'll know a lot about ourselves.'

We won by a point. Gooch scored that point in the second minute of injury time. There was controversy at the end. Declan was coming out with the ball and he got a bad old skelp and he reacted. It should be a hop ball, but the ref gives Declan a free and Seamus McEneaney, the Monaghan manager, is hopping mad. He goes on the field. I follow him. We exchange a few pleasantries out there. McEneaney makes a drive at me but doesn't make contact. The free leads to our winning point. Tomás tips it on to Eamon Fitz, who just rifles a cross-field pass to Gooch, who scores a classic point over the shoulder to win.

All hell breaks loose after the game. McEneaney's sidekick, Gerry McCarville, gets into a tussle with a linesman. He'll get suspended for that. We're out of there, though.

A year ago we lost by a point in Donegal in a tight one, and we left the place like lunatics. People would dismiss those games, but for us they were huge. The ones you win against the head, they make a team. You just look for that small bit of an edge, some sign of the hunger that we want. You triumph against adversity.

There was a great feeling in the huddle afterwards, standing out there, arm in arm, in muddy Scotstown. We'd stolen it. I reminded the boys of that game nine years ago. Maybe we'd turned the same sort of corner.

We needed to win like that, coming from behind in injury time. It feels significant. Hostile territory. Big crowd. People in on top of the pitch.

As a team we're still not flowing. A quick look at the report card: Gooch is off colour. Declan O'Sullivan was brilliant, fortunately. Mike Mac conceded three from play to Rory Woods. Darragh finished very strong. Aidan O'Mahony was good at number six.

Then Offaly came to Austin Stack Park on a cold night. We beat them, but we were poor. We were malfunctioning up front. The outside guys couldn't hit the inside men. It looked like the inside line wasn't showing. Gooch wasn't moving like he should. He was hanging back for the handy over-the-top ball into his arms. That's a very hard one to deliver under pressure. Darragh Ó Sé gave us a tour de force, but Diarmuid Murphy looked out of sorts in goal. Tomás Ó Sé got serious bother from Ciaran McManus and we had to put Aidan O'Mahony on McManus. Good news was that Mike Mac was awesome. He has reacted in the right way to criticism. I've been on his case since Monaghan. He looked like an All-Star full-back again. He'll need to show all that class next week on Stephen O'Neill.

Another consolation was that we had Paul Galvin back. Galvin has been the find of the past couple of seasons. He's my type of player and one of my favourite characters; but he's work sometimes, and he has a tendency to get in trouble on the pitch. In 2004 I'd dropped him for the Munster semi-final against Cork. I told him I couldn't trust him in the cauldron of Killarney. Back in the second league game of that year, after we'd got beaten in Longford, he got into fisticuffs with a Cork player at the end of the game in Tralee, and one of them ended up hitting Paul a dig to the side of the ear. It half knocked him out. There was a bit of bad blood over that. My worry was that all hell might break loose if I put him into the game.

He came on as a sub and did all right, and I put him in for the Munster final with Limerick and he flaked a fella. The next week we had an exchange on the phone about it. Exchange isn't really the right word. I was out on the lawn, roaring at him that he was giving me and the team a bad reputation. He was arguing back and making me more pissed off. Bridie was inside the window, putting the finger to her head and pointing at me, thinking I'd really gone mad at last.

In spite of these incidents he had a great season in 2004, which ended with him getting the one-thousandth ever All-Star Award. His club had gone on a run to the All-Ireland junior final. Then he ran out of steam. I remember one day late in the summer I was talking with him in training. He'd stopped positioning himself in training games, looking for breaking ball, and I was making some point to him and he more or less told me to fuck off. The edge was gone and he was frustrated.

Paul got taken off in the 2005 final. Then he got sent off in the North Kerry championship while playing for Finuge. He was involved in an incident in a game against Ballylongford in which a young fella called Liam Foley ended up with a broken jaw.

Galvin got suspended for six months by the North Kerry board. Life went on for the rest of us, and in the months after the All-Ireland final of 2005 life wasn't that great. The evening after the South Kerry final I got a phone call from Paul. I was at a low ebb. The year was over. Dromid had been beaten in the South Kerry final and Kerry had been beaten in September. There was no more adrenalin to run on. Paul had picked the wrong evening. I was cranky and queer and hungover and heading towards Ballin-skelligs, looking for somewhere to calm the nerves.

Paul was aggrieved. He told me that I wasn't looking after his suspension. I told him that I was all year tuned into him and his needs, all year looking for some little spark from him. I'm taking the time out now. I'm not on duty 365 days of the year. This is the second half of December.

He told me I wasn't tuned in enough. We were getting a bit cranky with each other, a bit insulting. I asked him, did it ever occur to him that he deserves it. He came back and said that Mickey Harte looks after his players when they are suspended, perhaps I should. He knows where to land the low blows.

Eventually I spoke to Mike Foley, who is Liam Foley's father and who held the whip hand in the whole suspension thing. If Mike said that he didn't mind the sentence being commuted, then the North Kerry board would commute. If not, if the Foleys wanted their full pound of flesh, then they were entitled to it.

When I made the call to Mike, I put it to him that he wouldn't be just doing Paul Galvin a favour, he'd be doing the county team a favour and he'd be doing me a favour. By this stage Galvin would have met with the Foleys, along with Sean Walsh. They'd have teased it out. Finally, on the Thursday before we played Offaly, there were a couple of months knocked off the suspension.

I've never met Mike Foley but we've spoken on the phone a couple of times since. It was big of him to give the word, and I hope the Kerry county board never leaves him short of an All-Ireland ticket.

Our man Galvin came back with a vengeance, fisting two points almost as soon as he came on against Offaly. The break did no harm at all to the hoor.

I know the job that Paul can do for us – I see him as the answer to a pile of worries. The game is about scavenging wing-forwards who dive in for the ball, fellas who work back. Trying to strike the right balance between aggression and control is what it's about. If Galvin gets the balance right this year, he'll be awesome. We've had rows, we've fought like cats and dogs, but he's invaluable. Somebody described him once as the poor man's version of Brian Dooher. I took exception to that cheap shot.

One thing I know about Paul is how he motivates himself. He keeps a little black book, like Jack Charlton used to do, and he writes down the name of anyone that's pissed him off on the pages of the black book. He writes down the names and why, and before he plays a game he takes it somewhere private and reads down through the pages, looking at those names, and promises himself he'll prove the bastards wrong.

I know my name is in there a few times at least. If it gets the best out of Paul Galvin, it's worth it.

8

By the middle of March we're four games into the National League and we have six points for our troubles. We have just one loss, to Mayo who, as we thought in Tralee, are flying at a very high altitude for this time of year. We've had a fierce battle in Scotstown which has been worth about twenty training sessions to us.

In my diary I scribble that we lack direction in our play and that Darragh is coming strong. I have a note that Donaghy needs to be tried at full-forward. I also write that I think that Mike Frank Russell has come to the end of the road: '*MF finished I think.*'

Mike Frank is one of my failures as a coach. As a player he has won everything. Colleges, club and county at every grade. I'm not sure anybody else in the history of the GAA has the same collection of medals that Mike Frank has. He's got Hogan Cup, minor, Under-21, senior, county, All-Ireland club. I didn't know if anyone else has ever done that.

I am sure of this, though: he won an Under-21 All-Ireland in 1996 and another in 1998, he won a senior in 1997, another in 2000 and another in 2004, and hopefully he is going to win yet another in 2006. I have been around for all of those. And Mike Frank and myself still don't understand each other. We'd have respect for each other, but I'm sure he has a bit of bitterness towards me.

When I meet Mike Frank I can never be sure if I am clicking with him. Maybe it reflects my own personality. I was a bit of a slogger as a footballer, and maybe I'd identify with the likes of Galvin, Guiney and Paddy Kelly a lot more. The Kerry public wouldn't see Paddy Kelly as a Kerry footballer in the classic sense. Or Galvin or Brendan Guiney. They'd be my men, though, hard bastards who'd go through walls for you. I can't get enough of those fellas around the place. They set the tone.

Mike Frank is introverted and very quiet. A truly nice fella, but just a very quiet lad. I can't understand him as a player and I can't reach him as a person.

In 2005 I made a mistake. I wanted him to fill the Johnny Crowley role and win some ball for us. I regret that. All the hours spent trying to get him to tackle and be a target man.

I went hard on him in training sessions. He wouldn't make the hard runs or contest the hard balls. He'd be waiting to feed off fellas and it drove me mad. What unnerved me about him was that he would be at his most exasperating when he was on the team. When he was off the team and trying to make it, he'd have a real cut at it. It was like he had a comfort zone when he made the first fifteen and he'd cruise. I had it in my head that what I'd see in the training sessions was what I'd pick the team on.

He's a lad who plays his own game. Myself and Johnny would be trying to get him to keep to his corner. Johnny would be very traditional that way. Next thing, Mike Frank would shoot away off somewhere else and Johnny would be shaking his head. 'Jack, there's nobody away in the left corner now. Where's he gone?'

I'd have met Mike Frank two or three times in the Bianconi in Killorglin for crisis meetings. I took him off to Rossbeigh beach for a spiel another time, back in 2004, coming close to the All-Ireland final when I was still trying to get inside his head. I needed to see where he was coming from. I do that with players. I met Seán O'Sullivan a week or two ago in Killarney one evening, just sat him down in the Park Hotel and told him I saw something different in him. He'd been peripheral in 2004 and then he'd gone to Australia in 2005. He'd beefed himself up in Australia and he'd come on in a few league games, and I liked what he was showing us. It's great to be able to touch base with fellas like that, give them the incentive and the spark.

I'd have spoken to the Killorglin club manager, John Evans, a few times about Mike Frank, just looking for the key to getting this man motoring.

A lot of people would feel that since Maurice Fitzgerald went off the scene we haven't seen Mike Frank at his best. Fitzie had a telepathy with him. He was the playmaker for Mike Frank's finishing. They were artists.

I remember in 2000, in the replayed All-Ireland semi-final with Armagh, Mike Frank kicked 2–3 from play.

I remember his first goal that day, late in the second half when we were trailing by two points. Maurice threaded a left-footed cross-field ball into Franny's belly button. It was an unbelievable pass. Franny turned, checked, and kicked a goal past two Armagh defenders. Rolled it into the corner. A fantastic goal.*

As the years went on he missed a ball-winner or a playmaker like Maurice Fitz. I think Mike Frank has said that. Back in 2002 he had a good understanding going with the Gooch, where the two of them would cross to each other's corner instinctively. Darragh was winning tons of midfield ball and popping it out towards those corners at that time. But things changed, and it seemed like we couldn't afford the Gooch and Mike Frank. With John Crowley we could flake it in. He'd fuck fellas out of the way and make a space.

At the end of the day, Mike Frank has ended up missing out

---

*Mike Frank's goal was the cue for one of the funniest incidents I've seen in my life. When we scored, Páidí ploughed up the sideline and ran into Brian McAlinden and said to him, 'Take that now, you bastard.' McAlinden had been annoying him all day on the line. Poor McAlinden received a good hefty shoulder into the back and got bowled over. There was ferocious tension out on the pitch, we'd gone a point up and all we could do was laugh.

Brian White had to come over before the start of extra time and he told Páidí to calm down. Up the line, McAlinden was pale as a ghost, just looking at the ground. I said to myself, for sure he'll go public and there'll be trouble, so I sidled up to him.

'Brian, pay no notice to that lunatic. He's mad.'

I thought no more about it till afterwards, when Páidí comes to me in the dressing room in his usual rig-out.

'Jack Hard, I heard what you said about me.'

'Who the fuck told you? I was just trying to calm him.'

I don't know whether Páidí is going to get thick or not.

He breaks into a big grin. 'The linesman came and told me,' he says, and off with him, happy as a lark around the dressing room, still bollock naked except for the boots on him.

starting in two All-Ireland finals under my management. Now I'm thinking that he's finished altogether. Maybe he feels that he's done enough. Maybe he feels he shouldn't be hacking himself any more.

Not getting selected in 2004 hit him very hard. He'd played in all the league games, but when it came to the crunch we just felt that John Crowley would give us savage presence near the Mayo goal. We'd noticed that Mayo liked to run the ball in the forwards and we knew their backs would have no practice under the high ball, so we went with Crowley in there and lamped in direct ball.

I spoke to Mike Frank's girlfriend on the night we came home after 2004. She told me that Franny couldn't understand why I had dropped him. We'd been close and through a lot together. In 1998 he was injured before the All-Ireland Under-21 final. He came back and trained for a week after being two months out, and I had said we'd take a chance on him because of his class. He made a goal with his first touch that day and kicked a great free, late on. I think Mike Frank would have thought that there was no way I would ever drop him.

It's hard because I know his family, who adore him. He's the shining light. The sitting room in Killorglin is like a shrine to Mike Frank's achievements. They were very hurt and I was *persona non grata* for a long time after that.

I've often looked back at the last two years and thought I was hard on Mike Frank. There's a stubborn streak in me, though. Others had the theory that he's a big game player and he wouldn't be hacking it too hard inside in training. It wasn't in my psyche to go down that road, though.

Last year we dropped him for the semi-final against Cork in favour of Bryan Sheehan. Mike Frank had kicked three points in the quarter-final against Mayo. Whatever happened to him in the training I don't know, but we weren't happy afterwards. We threw in young Bryan Sheehan for his first championship start. I got a text from Mike Frank that night: 'I want a meeting with you and the selectors after Sunday. I want to know why I was dropped off the team seeing as you as a manager didn't have the decency to give me a good reason.'

That's the first time I ever saw any anger from him, and it gave me some hope. I've never had a problem with a fella cutting loose at me. I'm always interested in what they'll come back with on the field.

I think Mike Frank expected to come back for the final. The evening that I told him he wasn't playing he didn't come down to the team meal or to the meeting. I saw it as a bit of a breach of faith. I'd be huge on that, sticking together. When I calmed down I rationalized it – I'm sure he saw my treatment of him also as a betrayal.

He sent me another angry text the next day. I sent him back an even angrier one. I half thought he'd walk off the panel.

I had a meeting with him up in the team hotel in Dublin, the day before the final. We agreed that Mike Frank would get tunnel vision and contribute what he could. He wasn't in the greatest frame of mind when he came on, and he wouldn't have been feeling much better when he finished.

Perhaps now he's had enough. The work we're doing on the tackle, on stopping fellas and on breaking tackles, it doesn't suit him. Going in to stop a man with his body, Mike Frank looks as awkward as spring harrow.

Maybe we're losing Mike Frank, but Seán O'Sullivan is a big plus. He kicked three from play in Monaghan, and that's a day we have spoken about a lot in the weeks since. It's a theme of ours. Backs to the wall. Finding a way to win. Pulling it out of the fire. Sean delivers a nice type of ball into the full-forward line, too.

We need to find a third man inside who will show for ball, though, or it's all academic.

We've had discussions with the chairman about flying up to the Tyrone league game, which is next. Getting there by road is a nightmare. After dodging and ducking a bit, he finally agreed that we would fly to Derry and get the coach down to Tyrone.

I had a meeting the other day in the Plaza with the Gooch. He hasn't been himself lately, and I wanted a word. We went for a swim and had a meal in the Park afterwards. He has such a great brain for the game but he's finding the whole scene claustrophobic.

Funny I've never been through that, but I know what he means. I remember coming up through Killarney early in 2004. I'd been to the afters of a wedding, following training. Bridie was driving and I was relaxing in the passenger seat and it was the early hours of the morning one night, in the middle of summer. There were people on the street, all over the street, having a good time. Young ones and guys sitting on the pavement, chatting each other up and drinking. I said to myself, how the hell does the Gooch keep his head in a town like this all summer long?

This man is a superstar. He's supposed to be at home in his bed while Killarney is partying. It's a huge demand on a young lad.

If I go to Old Trafford and watch the guys who make £80K a week, they drive past in their sports cars and home to their gated communities and that's their life. I like soccer, but there's more hitting and hurt in a week of Kerry training sessions than in a season with United. And the boys have 70,000 people roaring their names on Saturday afternoons while the Kerry boys have the lads with the narrowed eyes above in the stand cutting the legs out of them any time they play.

Everyone wants a piece of the Gooch. He works in the bank and people will walk right in and up to the counter just to take a look at him or to ask him something about football. He walks down the street and they want to talk about football. There are times when it gets to him. He wants to be a regular guy. It's hard. He works in Killarney. Lives there. Trains there. Plays for the club there. He's public property.

He says to me that the easiest part is training and games, because there's a wire between himself and the rest of the world. I've told him before that he needs two things: a car and a woman. He's got both now, a nice girl called Marguerite and some wheels. He can shoot out of town and get away from everything a couple of times a week.

I've got him access to the Plaza Hotel's gym. It's for guests only, so he won't be disturbed in there. I just felt it would be quieter there for him and it's straight across from work.

Of course I want something from him, too. I want the Gooch at his best. The bottom line, I tell him, is that it's six months to the All-Ireland. Tunnel vision. For great young players like Gooch or Declan you never know when the last chance will be.

The next night at training, the Gooch comes in looking very bright. There's a spring in his step. I can see some focus and energy in him. I'm pleased, but I know it's not me or my doing. We're heading for Tyrone. They have a hunger on them for Tyrone.

I'm pleased about the Gooch, but there's an article on the front of the *Kingdom* newspaper that's not so pleasing. The Kerry team is destroying club football, it says. Dara Ó Cinnéide, of all people, gives the impression that he fell out with me over club commitments before he retired. It makes me look like a right bollox.

I go home with a headache. One step forward, two steps back. Fuck them all.

PART TWO

Spring

9

Late March, and there is a poor atmosphere at training. I don't know why. We're at a critical juncture. We could sink or swim here. It's going to take work to turn this around, but the lads don't seem to see the urgency. I haven't slept well for the last few nights. This is not good. I need to relax. Mike Frank is cracking me up. He has been the best player at training, the last couple of nights. Jekyll and Hyde. What the hell?

The big thing I need to address is the issue of players who are hiding. We had a few on Sunday who were afraid to be exposed. A couple who stood off their men, pretending to be doing other things. Desperation stuff. Honest defenders must stand on their feet.

I send Dara Ó Cinnéide a text, explaining how disappointed I am with him over the *Kingdom* article. Dara was one of the players who got the county championship called off, back when he was captain in 2004. I play ball with the clubs. I'm off the head with rage. Grossly unfair. I encourage players, especially peripheral players, to play as much as possible with the clubs.

Dara rings me back and says he has been misquoted. Some galoot took excerpts out of what he'd said. I'm glad to see it's not Dara's fault, but it's an annoyance I could do without, as it gives the Kerry public another stick to beat me with. Dara makes a statement to the papers. We'll forget about it. Move on. Tyrone!

As the table lies, before we go to Tyrone we have eight points and they have four. They have a game in hand, but if we win they are out. So we're going to go for the jugular and lay down a marker. We're going to play Paul Galvin as an extra defender, play them at their own game and see what happens early on.

At the last training session before we move north, there's good focus in the team. We have a good session, plus some tactics and video. The emphasis is on moving the ball on and not getting caught in the tackle. Also work rate. I show the lads a snippet from the league game in Killarney last year, a day when we destroyed Tyrone. No harm to remind the team what we can do when we play football ourselves.

Sunday will be a big day for Mike Mac. Can he mark Stephen O'Neill? I'm starting to worry about our defence. I spoke to Tomás Ó Sé tonight about his lack of focus at the moment. He agrees he's not playing well but he is trying hard.

It might be a hangover from last year. Tomás wasn't playing well, going into the 2005 final. In training he wasn't getting tight on his man. We had a young fella called Mikey Collins in from Austin Stacks, and Collins was playing wing-forward, and every night Tomás was standing off him, not getting tight. He made Mikey Collins look very very good some nights. Looking back, Tomás didn't have a good start to the final, but he came strong in the second half and scored the goal that brought us back into the game.

I want more aggression. No more comfort zone. We talk about William Kirby putting the heat on Declan Meehan in the league final of 2004 to deny him a goal. We go back to Mike Mac, at the very end of the drawn All-Ireland final in 2000, staying with Derek Savage and forcing him on to his weak foot. If he didn't do it there'd be a few Kerrymen with one less All-Ireland medal today. It's inches.

The worst scenario in defence is to have to look at the player who is afraid to look bad. Tom O'Sullivan didn't get back on Canavan for the goal in the 2005 final. Canavan was his man, but Tom was off trying to look like he was doing something else, up-field supporting the play. Inches.

Tomás Ó Sé looked around him in the 2005 final to see where Ryan Mellon was gone instead of tackling Canavan. Inches.

In the 2004 championship versus Limerick, Mike Mac gave up on a ball to John Galvin. It finished in the net. In the Cork game weeks earlier, I'd seen Kevin O'Sullivan go around Mike, but that time he went after him and O'Sullivan fluffed his shot. Inches, boys. Lads, is anyone hearing a theme?

In the last month or so we've been working on the inches. The tackling work gets its real test when we play Tyrone. We've had tackle bags and fellas driving into them. We've seen senior footballers who are shy of physical contact and we've exposed them and worked with them.

If you listen in to one of our training sessions you just hear the same mantra. Break the first tackle. Break the tackle. Go at him. Break the tackle. Ride it out.

If you don't get through the tackle you're in trouble. We look at the video of the 2005 All-Ireland yet again. We were going laterally and Tyrone were fanning out across the pitch. They'll do that all day long.

The last entry in my diary before we head north is full of vim and vigour.

We're going to Omagh to play it honest and hard. Strangely this game is exactly what we need. Let's try our case. No hiding.

Tyrone 1–14, Kerry 1–12.

Beaten, but we learned a lot. We were four up, playing into the breeze, at half-time and playing measured composed football. We lost our way in the second half and they upped it for fifteen minutes and scored 1–5, including a great goal by Stephen O'Neill. So good a goal that I couldn't fault Mike Mac.

Two halves. We kept men back in the first half, and it worked. The lesson is to have the moral courage to do it for the full game The turnover ball cost us again, though. When we turned over ball from them, we didn't counter-attack at pace. We're still soloing into tackles.

Work rate excellent in first half. Must move the ball on at pace. Tackles.

Other problems? Of course there are. If you're going to find problems, it will be in Omagh against Tyrone.

Tom O'Sullivan threw in the towel a couple of times, fouling Martin Penrose when he needed to stay on his feet. Tom, along with Marc Ó Sé, Tomás Ó Sé and Eoin Brosnan, looked like they didn't want to try things. Marc was standing off Ger Cavlan. We need every player to be a presence.

Still, we fought hard and in the end we could have had a draw. Eoin Brosnan had a point over the middle of the bar and some fool waved it wide. Déjà vu. The crowd in Omagh was very hostile and on Sunday they pressurized the referee into marginal decisions. Given how tight the group will be, disallowing that point could prove to be a key critical error.

In the following week I find it hard to sleep. I make an effort to stand back and look at where we are going from the outside. I speak to a few of the lads who are not going particularly well. Tom O'Sullivan, I know, will come good. Marc Ó Sé gets so worked up, he goes off and plays a county league game which he isn't supposed to do because he's carrying an injury.

I pick up the *The Star* on Sunday and there's the bould Páidí having a go about our style of football. He'd do well to remember that he was the Kerry manager whose team kicked six points against Tyrone in the 2003 All-Ireland semi-final. I drop it and pick up the *Sunday Indo*. There's a huge feature on Páidí, the sexiest man in Ireland. Have to go out and get some air!

I've taken the weekend off after Tyrone, just looking for some perspective, and on Monday it comes crashing in. Mike Cooper, the Gooch's dad, drops dead at work. Although I'd known Mike to see for a few years, I never really met him until about ten days ago when we stopped for a chat. It was the first and last decent conversation I ever had with the man. He had the same unassuming manner as the Gooch and the same eyes. A lot going on in that head, I thought to myself.

Mike had been at a Crokes game, the day before he died. He was a devoted GAA man and a great clubman. His passing is a bad blow for the whole family. He was still a comparatively young man. I go up to the house with Johnny Culloty on Monday night. The Coopers live outside the town a little way. Nice, nice people.

I often meet Gooch's sister Geraldine at training or matches. They're a tight family, and Gooch being the youngest is going to feel it the most.

In cold football terms what it means is that we'll be without the Gooch on Sunday against Dublin. It's an opportunity to see what we can do without him. That's the positive way of looking at it. The other way of looking at it is to remember how good he was against Tyrone last weekend in Omagh. One of the top three games he has played for us. I'm learning not to worry, though, and just control the controllable.

For a while for the Gooch it must have seemed as if there'd be no real life to intrude on his fairy tale at all. He grew up with a football. Word would have reached us down in South Kerry about how good he was when he was fairly young. When Declan started going in to Killarney for underage Kerry teams, he'd come back with word of this skinny little kid called the Gooch who was literally unmarkable.

Declan was playing a schools final as the curtain-raiser on the day the Gooch made his debut for Kerry. He scored a goal with his first touch. Great players leave their card at the entrance.

Then, in the middle of the summer of 2005, he got the news about his friend Kieran Cahillane above in the dressing room after the quarter-final game against Mayo. Some of the boys had heard it that morning. Kieran and a few lads had been swimming early in the morning in one of the lakes around Killarney, and tragedy had struck.

Somehow the news was kept from the Gooch all day, and after the game Patrick Tatler from Killarney called him into the small room off the Croke Park dressing rooms and broke the news. Some of the Crokes lads went in to him.

I wasn't aware of it myself. Next thing, I saw Gooch with tears in his eyes and I asked him what was wrong. He told me. Jesus. His best friend. That was a tough, tough one for him. A brother of Kieran's, James Cahillane, had played Under-21 football for me and I'd have known the family.

(Young fellas. When I struck out on my own in 1998 with the

Under-21s, we had a young fella called Martin Beckett from the Crokes. He was just out of minor and he played wing-back with us that year. He was a blond lad destined for stardom, and he got killed in a car crash on the N7 that September, coming home in a car driving down from Dublin. A great kid and a huge loss.)

After Kieran's death the Gooch wasn't himself for a while. The spark was gone out of him. He wasn't enjoying the football. On the Wednesday before the All-Ireland semi-final against Cork, I got a notion to take him away out of Killarney. I rang him up and said, 'Colm, are you doing anything after work? We'll go for a spin.'

We headed out to Kenmare. Played seven holes of golf. Gooch has the most unusual grip on a golf club I've ever seen. He catches it so strange – but by God, can he play! He has this lovely co-ordination which he brings to everything. We shot our few holes of golf then headed over to Sheen Falls. We had a couple of pints. I wanted us to have a few drinks, to relax both of us. Then we went off to a bit of grub.

I knew him well enough by then. I could see the light was going out in him. He got talking, telling me that he was losing the kick. It just wasn't there any more. I told him the same. No point in me saying anything different, there was nothing for me to come on strong about. I was struggling, too.

He opened up a bit. You could see it was all affecting him.

I don't know why, but the Gooch cut loose the following Sunday against Cork in Croke Park. The best game he has had. After the match he sent me a text when we were coming down to Kerry again on the train: 'We'll have to go to the Sheen Falls again.'

It was nice. A way of connecting with him. That wasn't more than six months ago. Now he's had another blow.

It came into the equation to cancel team training on the Tuesday night, but we actually trained away because there was nothing going on. It was private at the Cooper house on the Tuesday. It might have been as well if we had cancelled.

I went ballistic in training over fellas being late out for the warm-up. There was the usual big crowd in the physio room, all the usual suspects, and I just lost it. I think there was a line drawn in the sand and it won't be happening again.

I'd noticed for a while that fellas were a bit casual coming out to training. There'd be a few lads inside in the old physio room; and half past six would come, and we'd be expecting them out then for training at quarter to seven, and ten to seven might come and there'd be stragglers still coming out.

So this evening in Fitzgerald Stadium the fellas have gone a bit dead and complacent. I've been saying to myself that we had to keep up the standards. So I let a roar.

'Lads, this is the last evening I want to see fellas inside in the physio room at ten to seven. Fuck it, c'mon. We're training two or three times a week for one and a half hours. I want thirty fellas out on the pitch. If you're not fit, fair enough; organize your physio in the off days if needs be, but this thing about wandering out – it's not on.'

There's a comfort factor in the physio rooms for a few fellas. Lads get used to it. Tommy Griffin would have a lot of niggling injuries, he got a bad one in 2004 when he looked like he'd go straight into the team for the quarter-final after coming on in the two Munster finals as a sub. He got a bad ankle ligament injury in training. Tommy would be a small bit careful since then.

I rang him one day and said, 'Fuck it, Tommy. Are you going to have a cut at this thing? If you are, then forget about the physio room and cut loose and we'll give you a go at it.' He spent a lot less time in the physio room afterwards. He was a revelation when he got into the team.

There's other lads. You'd be watching everything while you wait for them on the pitch. A few of the subs? Christ, you see them coming out late and you say, 'Jesus, lads, is this the way you're trying to impress us?' This thing about just strolling out creates a bad vibe about the place. I hate it.

We got training started anyway and I had a go then at Pat over some play-acting he was doing in training with the ball before the real football work started. Jesus. I'm trying to get them to knock lumps out of each other and Pat has them tipping around. He won't be doing that again either!

This is a week or so after Tyrone have run over us at the end of another game. Am I the only one who's edgy about that? To make matters worse, Mike Mac broke a bone in the hand tonight in a harmless incident. It never rains but it pours.

Of course I left some bad vibes of my own behind in Fitzgerald Stadium. While I was driving home, Declan rang me. There were grumbles back from the players.

I told Declan that I didn't give a fuck what the players thought of me, that was the way it was going to be.

Sarah Hobbs, our physio, rang me on the way home, too. It's not her fault, although she thinks I'm blaming her. We had it out, anyway. This *craic* must stop. The situation cannot continue. There's an onus on me to get the fellas out the door and training on time.

Now and then, to be honest, I would imagine every county manager gets a bit pissed off over this. You get a message that somebody is able to play football but not to do the running. Why? Is it swimming they'll be doing when they play the football? Is there not some running involved there?

Something doesn't sound quite right. You listen to that a couple of nights, and it goes around your head. So the rule has to be that if you can't train you can't play football either.

Fellas start moaning otherwise. That guy doesn't want to hack himself with the physical stuff, he wants to spare himself for the football. Lads notice. You hear them saying that they were marking that bollox in training and he did no work all night, and then when there's a game at the end he's running around like a madman with the ball.

You have to watch it for the team's benefit. That's my excuse tonight, anyway.

Everyone is pissed off with me all of a sudden. I don't care. We have Dublin coming to town on Sunday. It's time everyone stood up to be counted. We're looking at going on the pitch this Sunday without Gooch and Mike Mac, maybe our two best players.

We are all going to have to get more aggressive and focused. Up the ante. If they're all pissed off, so be it. That's a start.

10

On your own for a while you turn selfish. Is Colm really gone for Sunday, you wonder. Even to have him along would be a boost for us all.

I touched base with the Gooch. If he felt like coming up, he was to come up. On the morning of the match I called him and asked him how he felt. He'd talked about it to his family, and his mam felt that his dad would have wanted him to go up for the game.

So the Gooch was with us for the game with the Dubs. He did the warm-up. I asked him how he was. Not too bad. I assumed the adrenalin was keeping him going. He'd slept very little.

We were in a bit of bother, ten or fifteen minutes into the second half. We looked towards the Gooch. He nodded. I asked him to warm up. He electrified the place. When he came on we were two points down. He got a point with his first touch. We scored four points in a row. We got a draw out of it. Thirteen points each. I'm happy with that. When we warmed down in our usual corner of the field I thanked Colm, and the players gave him a round of applause. It felt better that he'd come down and that he played today.

When I got home, other things were playing in my head. A simple stat. Kerry six wides. Dublin thirteen wides. We were steeped to draw the game. Diarmuid Murphy saved a penalty, but they had two other goal chances as well. We were wiped out in midfield. Donaghy got tossed around by Shane Ryan. Darren Magee gave Darragh a hard time, too.

Mayo and Tyrone drew in Castlebar, so we go through by a single point. It's poetic justice. Eoin Brosnan had that perfect point disallowed up there in Omagh because the crowd were howling like banshees.

We had Seamus Moynihan back against the Dubs. That's the biggest positive I could have wished for. I remember him coming off towards the end of last year's All-Ireland covered in sweat, having had a hard time, down on himself, and he thought and I thought it was the end. He was in pain, and mentally he was beating himself up.

In November he started doing serious core stability work with Ger Hartmann in Limerick. His back problems cleared. He put himself through a private hell over the winter in order to come back. At times, he says, he thought he'd only play club football again, but I know Seamus Moynihan. The Pony wants one last crack at this.

I left him to be doing his own thing and we kept in contact by phone. He came back in for a challenge game against Kildare a few weeks ago, but it was a bitter cold day and not long after he came on at half-time he tweaked his hamstring and was gone again.

Last Wednesday, though, the day after Mike Mac broke his finger, Seamus and I talked. We had a vacancy. We needed him to fill it. Now he's back. There's no team that wouldn't be better with Seamus Moynihan in it.

I remember the 2000 All-Ireland semi-final replay against Armagh, for instance. He got a rough time from Oisín McConville in the first half. He knew it, too. In the second half he was like a one-man band. For about fifteen monutes when Armagh came at us he was holding them off single-handedly. Hitting guys, leaving his own man, covering for others. It was a phenomenal display. For mental strength they haven't invented the animal that would beat Seamus Moynihan for seventy minutes.

My third game in this job was in Parnell Park against Dublin. We hadn't won a league game there in eighteen years, and at six points down at half-time it didn't look like we were going to win that afternoon either. Conal Keaney took three points from play off Seamus in the first half. When you are a new manager and you see Seamus Moynihan being taxed for three points in a half, you begin to wonder if you're in the right job.

In the second half Seamus ran the whole show. He even scored the point that gave us the lead, a minute or so from the end. We tacked another two on for a famous win. I can't say I knew then that we'd win the All-Ireland, but I knew I had Seamus Moynihan on my side and we'd taken a big step forward.

Back in 2004 I just couldn't be sure where I stood with the Gaeltacht boys. I remember that after their exploits with the club they rejoined the squad for the league semi-final against Limerick. We chose to go to the Gaelic Grounds to play that game as we were going to have to go there in the summer anyway. That week I got a call from a friend who is a referee. He quietly tipped me off that Darragh's name had come up a few times at referees' meetings and that he was being watched this season. The advice was to tell Darragh to keep his nose clean until the heat died away.

I went to Darragh and gave him the word. I could tell that for some reason he didn't believe me. That day against Limerick he got himself into a spot of trouble, and the referee gave him bother for it. It was hard not to say, 'I told you so, Darragh!'

As the 2004 season turned out, we won the All-Ireland final virtually without Seamus or Darragh. Seamus came back for a run in the final. Darragh couldn't play as he was injured. I think somewhere along the line, perhaps after 2005, Seamus and Darragh decided that they need to go and win one last All-Ireland for themselves.

We play Laois in the league semi-final. After that, Darragh and his brother Marc are leaving for a week to attend Dara Ó Cinnéide's wedding in New York. I'll know by the state of the pair of them when they come back to what extent they have bought into the plans for 2006. It's not that they haven't given it everything in terms of commitment for the past two years. It's just that I don't know that they have committed fully.

Declan Coyle, who is our official supplier of positive thoughts, tells a story about commitment. It involves the Moors landing in Spain for the first time. Just 7,000 of them on a beach in the south of this strange country which, they know, has a huge army. They're standing on the beach with their boats and their lives behind them and their leader gets up on a platform and addresses them.

He asks the 7,000 if they are committed. As usual when you ask any group if they are committed, there is a big cheer. Yes, they are committed. He asks again. The cheer is bigger this time. Of course they are committed.

'All right,' he says, and he gives the order to burn the boats.

I know the Sé's are here on the beach with us. I know what they are worth in the battle. But I don't know yet if they've committed to the extent of burning those boats.

Last year in the run-up to the Tyrone game in the league, the fourth Ó Sé brother, Fergal, got married. It was a big occasion for the lads, and Darragh was best man. The boys went back west for the do naturally, and for a week Darragh didn't come back. We may be remote in South Kerry, but news travels fast. Great tales reached me every day of the drinking being done up in Ard a Bhothair in Ventry. I know enough to know that the stories were exaggerated, but when Darragh rang me on Saturday to tell me he had a bit of an old bug and wouldn't be at his best on Sunday, I began to put two and two together.

We were playing Tyrone. A big deal of a game for us at any time. I told Darragh on the Sunday morning to just stay at home. It was a confrontation I knew I would win. That's why I chose it. (Darragh's absence let in Liam Hassett, who became one of our main men that summer.)

Early the next week Darragh and I had a meeting and a meal in the Bianconi in Killorglin. No tempers or voices raised. I told Darragh that we'd beaten Tyrone without him at the weekend and that we'd won an All-Ireland final without him the previous September. It was up to him. I don't know if I convinced him. That wasn't the point, anyway. I wanted his enthusiasm, not his obedience.

I'd known it would be hard for Darragh, Tomás and Marc to buy in straight away to what we were trying to do. They are a close family and had worked with Páidí for years. It hadn't ended well, and they must all have felt the hurt.

I have an old buddy, Jerry Mahony, who I turn to for counsel and comfort and a few pints every now and then. Jerry knows people and he knows the game.

Jerry always told me to hang in there with the Ó Sé boys. 'Anyone could train twenty-four Seamus Moynihans,' he'd say. 'Wilkinson couldn't handle Eric Cantona. Ferguson could.'

Darragh never took me on head-to-head, but he'd test me in team meetings. I'd be on about tactics. Darragh would say, 'Why can't we just kick the ball out and fight for our ball?'

(To me, against the big northern teams that's playing into their hands, making a war of attrition out of it. In 2000 Darragh had Armagh's Cathal O'Rourke coming in from the wing at kick-outs and cutting in front of him to take his run away. He never got off the ground. A couple of us selectors actually went behind Páidí's back before the 2000 replay. We went to Declan O'Keeffe, our goalie. Deco was told to put a few kick-outs in the direction of Mike Hassett, who would be marking O'Rourke. The idea was to make O'Rourke stay put, to keep him honest. Páidí would never yield to that. In west Kerry they have the tradition of the *fear laidir*, and Darragh was our *fear laidir*. Kicking the ball away to somebody else was a sign of weakness to Páidí. We couldn't show any weakness.)

As a player and as a man, Darragh would have absorbed a lot of the *fear laidir* culture. The whole thing with Declan Coyle, for instance, has always irritated him. I saw Declan's name a couple of times in connection with sports psychology work he had done with other teams, especially Down, and I got his number. The day I rang Declan for the first time, he happened to be in Cahirciveen for the first time in his life. He worked with me personally in 2004 and then with the players in 2005, and now he works with us not as a group but with myself and some of the players as individuals. He keeps us positive.

Darragh tells me that Declan has no business inside with the team. I tell him that, just because it doesn't work for Darragh Sé, doesn't mean it won't work for others. Declan works well for some lads. Some players, you need to be telling them twelve hours a day that they are great. If that's what it takes, so what. As a manager you have to cater for everyone. Páidí built the dream on Darragh. Not intentionally or out of favouritism; it's just that the west Kerry culture predominated. The *fear laidir*. The strong man who does his talking on the field. The younger lads from elsewhere were half intimidated by the aura, I think!

Myself, I tread on eggshells. When I want Darragh to play differently I have to plan my attack. The game now is more about winning the breaks than winning the high catches. So I'd be saying to Darragh, 'Tap it down, like in a rugby line-out. Don't be catching the fucking thing at all.' He wouldn't be impressed. So I'd have to put it in a way that appears more positive. 'Look to break it to Tomás or to Moynihan. They'll get the ball on the burst and be gone like a shot.' Darragh goes for that more.

Sometimes, the boys are a law unto themselves. In 2005, when things were flat and we weren't feeling the edge, we did a couple of those bonding exercises. They're like fast food; they fill you for a while, but there's no nourishment. At the time, though, we needed filling.

One day we went up the lakes of Killarney in rowing boats as far as Lord Brandon's cottage and then we walked through the Black Valley. Seven miles or so of a hike together. I know that two of the Ó Sé's who were present, Darragh and Tomás, went to the bottom of the lakes, cut through the near route over to the Kenmare Road, and got somebody to pick them up to take them down to Killarney! This hike was something we were supposed to do as a team, everybody together. That was the principle. The two boys vanishing left everyone else feeling a bit stupid.

It wasn't the right thing to have a confrontation over, though. I hopped an old ball about it instead. I was talking later about a possible team trip out to the Skelligs. Somebody asked why the Skelligs, and I said that at least the Ó Sé's won't be jumping overboard.

They're the Sé's, though, and you make allowances. As Jerry Mahony would say to me, it's only bullshit. They'll do it between the white lines for you. He was right. Tomás Ó Sé was national

Player of the Year in 2004. Marc could have been Player of the Year in 2005 if we had won the All-Ireland. They win All-Stars. What manager wouldn't want to keep them onside?

It doesn't matter if you have a guy who is the nicest fella in the world and a fancy footballer to boot. A player like Darragh is undroppable by comparison. When Nicholas Murphy wants to put it up to Kerry, it's not the nice guys that will stand him down. Darragh's a competitive hoor. Put it up to him, he'll give it back. Some players are handy men to have when you're five points up. There's others, when you're two points down you want to see them attacking the game and taking it by the scruff of the neck. Darragh is one of those. A man for the trenches.

Jerry Mahony has always told me that it is my weakness as a manager that I had to like a fella to rate him. I've changed. I've always rated the Sé's. As time goes on I like them more and more, too.

Before I can start worrying about Darragh and Marc in New York, we have to face Laois. We have decided to drop Eoin Brosnan and to start Bryan Sheehan at the weekend. It's just a wake-up call for Brossy. He hasn't being going well. We're also dropping Mike Frank. I'm frustrated, just looking at him. We're thinking of dropping Tom O'Sullivan for Killian Young. There's something happens with Tom every year, and I feel it coming soon. Tom has started acting the maggot.

Diary entry:

Saturday 15th April: Fierce cranky during week. Whatever happens, I don't want Dwyer to beat me!

No need to worry! We trained well as a team through the week, just a couple of those sessions when you can feel a squad pulling together. The week finishes in an eight-point win against Laois. The lads reckon Laois are going nowhere. Pat looked at their legs before the game and announced that we'd win well. Laois had been doing too much running, he said.

Can't say I didn't have a little smile on the sideline, seeing

Micko suffer on his return to Kerry. He's put me through the wringer a few times.

The league finished well for us. Darragh and Marc came back from New York in fine fettle. If they had a couple of glasses of wine for the week, I'd say that was it. They looked great. For the first time I felt that we were all pulling the same way.

We beat Galway in the league final without much fuss or fanfare. We shared the weekend with the Munster v. Leinster rugby match and we went under the radar. Fewer than 8,000 at the game on a Sunday evening in Limerick!

Galway started better, with men behind the ball and using a crowded defence. It was awful to watch. We were in a bit of disarray, and Galway were trying to be Tyrone Light. We had no width or movement inside. We got caught between carrying it and kicking it. We brought Darren O'Sullivan on for Ronan O'Connor before half-time and Brossy on for Eamon Fitz at half-time. I cut loose a bit with the tongue when the fellas came in for the break, and in fairness they stood up afterwards.

One big difference straight away. No more stupid kicking. Brosnan ran at Blake and forced him out. They had to come out and mark Brosnan properly. This freed the Gooch up. Darren gave us some width. We won by 2–12 to 0–10, having been three points down at half-time. Our backs wiped out those great Galway forwards, and Darragh Ó Sé was awesome in the second half. A man possessed.

Not bad. A year previously, out of the league and listless, we'd gone up to play Kildare in Naas on league final weekend. Some of our boys had been piling back into the City West Hotel from Copperface Jack's the next morning just as the Armagh team were getting ready to go and play the final from the same hotel.

This felt much better. I ordered a week off for everyone. We all needed some rest and recreation.

One of the advantages of being the youngest in a family the size of ours is that the worst is over by the time you come along. All the hardships and sacrifices have been made and a lot of whatever is left over goes into spoiling the last of the brood. For that reason, when I finished secondary in Scoil Uí Chonaill in Cahirciveen I was the first of the family to get the chance to go to college.

My sister Caít, who was reared by our Aunt Kate, went for a small bit of third level, but I was the first full-time academic prospect as such. My mother was a frustrated teacher. Her own teachers had told her parents that she should have been sent to training college, but back then they hadn't the price of it. So it was special for her that Johneen was going off to Maynooth.

Not that the family could afford to see me to the station and give me a going-away ceremony using pound notes as confetti. My financial situation was that I worked that summer, picking stones on a farm back in Aughatubrid. A farmer called Johnny Griffin paid me £10 a week through the summer of 1978 and I headed to Maynooth with the princely sum of £60 in my pocket.

I got a grant, too. £1,000 for the year, or £333 per term. I stayed with my brother Paddy in Leixlip and cycled to Maynooth and back every day. I'm sure there was a party scene somewhere, but for me it was a fairly serious few years. After a while I moved to Joe, my other brother's, house and lived with him for two and a half years.

The last year, when I was doing teaching practice in Scoil Catriona in Glasnevin, I lived in Maynooth and caught the train across the city. It was a hard-working, uneventful time. I came home for the summers usually and played football and worked. I had a summer in London and a summer in New York, working.

After graduating, the first job I got was teaching down in Waterville for a year. I was teaching on the same staff as the Bomber Liston. We worked together, and one summer we soldiered together in New York, playing for the Clare club.

I don't know if I ever had serious notions about playing for Kerry when I was younger, but I certainly would have had the ambition to play for South Kerry. I played to a reasonably good standard at that level. In Maynooth I was lucky. Father Gerald McAleer of Tyrone trained the Sigerson Cup team, and again I came under the influence of a coach who taught me a lot.

Back home, I think Mick O'Dwyer had stopped looking after Waterville when I played for them in a South Kerry final in 1984. Dromid wouldn't have been within an ass's roar of a South Kerry final, and by then I'd fallen out with the club anyway. I hadn't yet learned enough from other managers.

I was always fairly single-minded, and although I wasn't the only man in Dromid who cared about football it would be fair to say that I was the one who cared the most. I was training Dromid when I was about nineteen or twenty years old. Nobody else would do it, and probably I would have let nobody else do it anyway.

The trouble was, nobody else had the same ambition. One year we went up from Division Five to Division Four, and we thought all our Christmases had come together. We won the first game the next season and then lost the rest. Same old rubbish.

I was obsessed, though. I was hard on lads. It was, as they say, my way or the highway. Some of the lads were happy enough with the highway. One night, one of the boys wouldn't do what I was telling him to do at training. I wanted him to play in goal. He wanted to play out the field. We had a row. He thought I'd got pretty high-and-mighty. One night not long after, he bumped into me at a disco. We were out the back of Tom Keane's ballroom, at The Ringside Rest in Cahirciveen. He hit me a couple of pokes and asked me who the fuck did Jack O'Connor think he was all of a sudden. There was no good answer to that question!

I went back to the club the next week and I told them, back me or back my assailant. This was more controversy and drama than the club was used to and they sat on the fence, hoping the whole thing would go away. Instead, I went away. I said, that's it. I'll get out of here, and I went down the road and played with Waterville for three years.

I've got plenty of slagging about it since, but at the time I just wanted to play football with fellas who took it as seriously as I did. It was a stupid row though, and I learned my lesson. I was too cranky and dogmatic with fellas. I was the wrong man. I was too driven. I was giving out too much for fellas and they got sick of me. You have to pick your fights. If you're going to have a row with a fella, always make sure it's a row you can win.

That South Kerry final of 1984 would have caused a few smiles around Dromid. I went off to work in London that summer and came home to play in the game. We were beaten by St Mary's by a couple of points. A Jack O'Shea rocket from about thirty yards out did for us. I was in the same jersey as Jack when our divisional team, South Kerry, got to the county final that year, too. We were beaten by a very dubious decision when playing Páidí Ó Sé's crowd from out west. Páidí got the captaincy for West Kerry out of that game. One of our men, John Galvin, was coming out with the ball in injury time and the game was tied at eight points all. He was pulled for overcarrying the ball. They scored. Nine points to eight. Here's the captaincy of Kerry for you, Páidí. I've never seen a player as disappointed as Jack O'Shea was after that game.

I had other fish to fry, though.

I met Bridie Moriarty in the Lobster Bar in Waterville in 1982. It's always feast or famine! I had a date with another woman that night and, looking back, the other woman could say she had a lucky escape. She went by the wayside when I saw Bridie. My first date dug her heels in a bit, but so did I. Being reared up in Toorsaleen we were deprived of women. When you saw a good one, you knew what to do.

I was teaching Bridie's sister, Geraldine, so I knew the family.

Bridie happened to be at a loose end and, even though I wasn't strictly free to be thinking such a thing, I noticed straight away that she was a bit of all right.

Our first proper date was in the Crock of Gold in Killarney, an old haunt which has since disappeared. I was doing a diploma in, of all things, catechetics. I'm half heathen but I thought the diploma was going to help me to get a teaching job. Irish and English were my subjects, but if I added something else to my little bag of tricks I might get a shot at a permanent job.

I was fairly half-hearted about the trips to Killarney for the catechetics evenings until Bridie came along. Bridie was working in the Great Southern at the time and her being in Killarney gave me the incentive to finish the course – or at least to drive to Killarney a few times a week with half a mind to finish the course. It was a fair spin in to Killarney and a fair spin home again on the nights I made it home. That's catechetics for you, though.

We were going out for about four years before we decided to hit the States together. My name came out of the hat in a draw for the Donnelly visas. It was 1986 and the rest of our lives were going to be the same as our lives were then unless we struck out and did something different for a few years. We said we'd give New York a try. I ditched teaching. Bridie by then was working in Tralee General. She threw in that job and we hightailed it off to the New World.

My Uncle Jack lived up in Seaman Avenue in the upper tip of Manhattan in a neighbourhood called Inwood, just a mile or so from Gaelic Park. I was going to do something unusual for an Irishman in New York. I was going to work construction. Bridie got a job very near us in the Tara Gift Shop at Inwood.

New York is all about connections. For a while I lived with my uncle and Bridie lived with a Cork girl, Eileen Kingston, who was going out with my uncle's son, Timmy. Before I knew how to bang a nail into a piece of wood I was a proud member of the Carpenters' Union, the 608. The official name was the United Brotherhood of Carpenters and Joiners of America.

Having a green card, I was able to reverse a trend. I played football in Gaelic Park under my own name and often I even worked under my own name. Occasionally I worked under another name if casual jobs came up, usually calling myself Benny Walsh. The real Benny Walsh was one of my employers. He ran the Inisfree Bar, where I put down a fair few hours. On one job somebody learned my real name, and for a while in Irish circles in New York I was known as Jack Benny.

When we'd been there a while we got to know another Irish couple who were on the verge of a move home. The girl, Debbie, was the daughter of Paddy Fogarty, the chairman of the Waterville club, and she was going out with a fella called Padraig Clifford. They were heading back to Ireland, so we took over their apartment in Bainbridge Avenue, right in the hub of the Irish community in the Bronx. That's where we hung out, meeting as many Kerry people in a day as we would have at home.

For a few years in New York I worked like a dog. Mad hours. Construction during the day, the Inisfree Bar at night. There was as much work as you wanted. One St Paddy's Day I worked the construction until around three in the afternoon. Then there was a buddy of mine and his brother owned a famous bar called Rosie O'Grady's in midtown Manhattan, a big favourite of the Kerry and Dublin lads from the 1970s. He brought me down there to do the door for a few hours for a hundred bucks. I went home, showered, had a bite to eat and went and worked in the Inisfree till four in the morning. Money coming at me from all angles.

Sometimes a great notion, as the song says . . . I got one of my better ideas around then. I had been working for this scaffolding company called Atlantic Scaffolding and I'd met up with another fella as mad for work as myself. The two of us decided that as we seemed to work a few times faster and harder than everyone else, it would pay us to take work off Atlantic Scaffolding on price. We worked like demons. It paid Atlantic Scaffolding to pass work on to us and pay us a good chunk of what they were getting. We earned more than we would have on the normal payroll.

We organized two crews and drove them hard. We'd lamp up a hundred foot of scaffolding a day, where it was taking the regular boys a week to do the same. Atlantic Scaffolding was getting jobs done a lot faster and we were getting a lot more money than a regular weekly wage.

It was hard, dodgy work at times. Down around Park Avenue or Fifth Avenue it was always like working in the middle of a crowd coming out of Croke Park on All-Ireland day. The eight-foot bridges we had to build were fine; the sixteen-footers were dangerous. You had to put this razor wire on top to keep the crazies from coming in on top of it.

There were other dangers, too. I was working late one evening on a scaffold, thirty-four floors up above a Manhattan street. I had a bottle of Gatorade which I was keeping for my break, and when I reached for it I had sweat on my hand and the bottle slipped. I watched it sail out and down like a two-pound crock of jam and I knew in my head that it could kill somebody. It was the most I could do to keep looking at it and not turn straight away and flee to JFK Airport. The bottle hit the ground about two feet in front of a yellow cab.

Life changed. In New York, Bridie and I got married in the Good Shepherd Church near where my uncle lived. We honeymooned down in Orlando.

Some time later I was up on a scaffold at seven in the evening when I got a call to go to the hospital in Englewood, New Jersey. Our eldest son, Cian, was born there at twenty past four in the morning. A couple of hours later, Bridie was up and decided to go for a walk and leave me with Cian. There's a famous photo in the family, taken when Bridie came back from her walk: me fast asleep with Cian hugged to my chest like a football. Poor soul, I don't think he ever trusted me too much after that.

We got this romantic notion one day around then. News came through from home that they were building a church in Dromid. There was an opportunity here. We decided that any place that would have a church would have a pub. And we hoped that any place with a pub would have a shop. And if a place had a church and a pub and a shop, it might develop as a community. And if it developed as a community, it might begin to take its bloody football seriously. And if it did that, I would go home and play before I was too old.

So my brother Mike and I decided we'd be the ones to build the pub and the shop. I flew home to help Mike buy the plot.

Bridie and her sister, Noreen, dropped me to JFK. I landed back in the other world that is Toorsaleen the next day and the phone rang early. Bridie was asking me what registration number our car was. (I had bought it recently, a Toyota Corolla estate. I'd seen it for sale one evening on Bainbridge Avenue, with a phone number stuck in the window. I lifted the phone and recognized the voice after a few seconds. A fella I went to school with, John Kissane.) Bridie had parked the car outside the door. Next time she stepped out, it was gone.★

★Funny enough, the next car I bought, after coming back to New York, had a bad end too. I was talking with Mike on the phone about the pub and ran late one day. We used to train up in White Plains and I went out of the house in a mad rush, driving up Jerome Avenue, where I flaked the car in the direction of some cab. The driver coming across swerved and the back of my car skidded. There was a bit of damage to the back of my car.

I thought nothing of it until I was coming home on a Friday evening a week later, heading up from the city, and I got a powerful smell of smoke. I opened the window of the car at the traffic lights and a cab driver pulled up beside me at the lights. 'Fierce fire somewhere,' I say to him. 'Do you smell that smoke?'

He just looks at me and shakes his head.

On we go. The smoke is getting worse. Next thing, I'm going north on the Henry Hudson Parkway under the George Washington Bridge and a car is flashing its lights at me. It's a Friday evening. Two lanes going north, two south on the highway. I look in the mirror and there's flames coming up out of the boot.

I pulled in. Nobody could pass the car. A mile of traffic jam straight away. I ran at first, thinking the thing would explode, then I remembered that all my tools were in the car. I couldn't go without the tools! I went back, opened up the boot and everything in there was on fire.

Now some Puerto Ricans had pulled out of the traffic and they were shouting at me. They were getting handfuls of sand and dirt and throwing them on the fire. We all started throwing the sand in, and after a few minutes we put out the fire. I thanked them, and in a fit of insanity and embarrassment I sat down in my half-melted car and drove it off back home to Bainbridge Avenue, three

Meanwhile, back in Kerry, Mike and I bought the plot of land up the road from the new church in Dromid. Then I flew back to New York and Mike did all the work. He broke his hand back while building the pub. He got a cast put on it and went on working.

The plan was that when everything was ready for opening, Bridie and I would come to Dromid for a fortnight to help get the bar up and running. A friend drove us to JFK and I told him when exactly he'd have to be back to pick us up.

With the opening of its first public house, Dromid went pure mental. We called it the Inny Tavern after the river that ran behind it. People supported it massively. There must have been lot of old money in Dromid taken out from under mattresses or floorboards or somewhere. Everyone in the area would come, and a lot of outsiders, too. There was no mention back then of the bag or blowing into it, and for young people and the old-timers the Inny Tavern was a social centre. They didn't have to be finding a corner in a bar in Waterville or Cahirciveen. They had their own place.

The return of Bridie and myself to Bainbridge Avenue was postponed again and again, and after a couple of months we knew there'd be no going back. The Inny Tavern was a centre for darts leagues, dancing, music sessions, pool competitions. It was packed from opening to closing and then sometimes for a few hours after closing.

It was a great time in our lives. I still remember coming home on 23 October 1989 and driving down to the bar. I had seen the field when we bought it, and now there was the house, the bar and the shop sitting there in front of me. This was before the Celtic Tiger and it was the only bit of building done in the Dromid region that year. I was going to be living above the shop and I walked in as they were putting the finishing touches to things. My Uncle Timmy was doing something with a worktop. I had my trade union card and I pulled it out and asked loudly if everyone

---

or four miles away! I drove it around the corner, took off any identification and left it there. Within a week it was picked clean by the vultures!

on this job was Union because I was here from the United Brother-hood of Carpenters and Joiners of America.

Without any pause a voice said, 'You wouldn't join your fucking hands, you clown.'

We were home.

12

Early May. The things you do for football. I'm throwing handfuls of ice from the Sam Maguire on top of a male model in an ice bath in Croke Park. There's a posse of photographers clicking and a gang of journalists laughing. Some carry-on.

These press conferences to launch the various competitions of the GAA are getting to be a ritual. You get thrown a few bob in expenses and brought up to Dublin to toss out a few old clichés. Throw some ice on a male model and get the picture in the paper, and everyone is happy, apparently.

The gang was all there. Paul Caffrey being his usual wary self, talking the Dubs down, no matter what got said. Peter Ford looking a bit chastened after what happened to Galway in the league final. Mickey Harte, of course. He's looking downbeat after Brian McGuigan's leg break. Who wouldn't be?

Being in Croke Park makes me think. We want to get back to this place quickly. We need to tune in now and stay focused. When we came back to training last night, the lads had lost some sharpness.

Here's what we managers always say: it's good to let them get back to clubs, the players are fresher coming back! Here's what we say to each other on occasions like Croke Park: like fuck. They're zombies when they come back. It takes a week to tune them back in again. The clubs are more relaxed. They're with old company they grew up with and they know they can come down a gear and relax. They come back to county training and it's hard to get them tuned in again.

I hate the period between the end of the league and the start of the championship. With respect to Waterford or Tipp, you know the lads won't be straining at the leash in training. We've just finished the league and played Tyrone, Dublin, Galway and

Laois. And now at training they are as dead as dodos. And I am supposed to shout at them that, if things don't improve, Waterford will beat us!

There's a pile of queer stuff in the weekend papers as they look forward to the summer. Sean McGoldrick in the *Sunday World* has me as the national favourite for the chop. I'm ranked 9.9 on a scale of 10 measuring the pressure managers are under. Thanks, Sean.

We've just won the league, haven't we? The lads got hold of the *Sunday World* after training one evening. Nine point nine out of ten for pressure, Jack! Great laugh.

In the rest of the previews all the usual suspects join with Micko and tip Tyrone for the All-Ireland. Call me paranoid, but I'm beginning to think Liam Hayes has it in for us. I'll be watching him carefully now this summer with Carlow. There's obviously a lot I have to learn.

We've had a meeting in Johnny's house and came up with a plan for dealing with this weird period of the year. We decided to get some fun into training, not be too heavy-handed too early.

I was in good form at the meeting and it all sounded good. When I'm out walking or running, though, I'm thinking of the one thing only. The need to break tackles in order to put good ball in. I watched Declan O'Sullivan playing at number ten in a club game last Saturday night. He didn't do badly there. He's strong. For a wing-forward, going across the pitch with the ball is a waste of time. Despite the talk about fun, I decided to push the drills for breaking tackles all the more. We also work hard on moving the ball faster. The more you slow the ball, the more chances you give the opposition to organize.

One night after training in the week before the Waterford game I show the lads clips from the league campaign: all these great scores that came when we moved the ball on quickly. I'm trying to get this message across so we have a system that everyone buys into. They all seem happy.

★

Kerry v. Waterford, Sunday, 21 May, Killarney.

Christ, what a day. We went eight points to two up and tried to coast all the way home. We were eight points to five ahead at half-time and there was an epidemic of fellas not working or covering. So I read the Riot Act at half-time.

We went back out and we were worse, if anything, at the start of the second half. Waterford missed a penalty, which should have been like an electric shock to us. We still couldn't raise our game, though. We took off Eamon Fitz and Eoin Brosnan after fifteen minutes of the second half. Again Darren O'Sullivan made a difference, but even the Gooch was very bad out there. We took him off in the second half, too. Paul O'Connor was promising when he came on. He kicked a great score. In the end we won by eight points.

Afterwards I went nuclear in the dressing room. Attitude problem! Unacceptable! Never seen worse!

Pat Flanagan spoke and blamed our preparation. The county board have been putting on club matches and we've been training out in Fossa instead of Fitzgerald Stadium for a little while as well. The stadium is being re-sodded. Pat mentions these things.

Sean Walsh feels that Pat is having a go at him over the playing of club matches. Sean runs out of the door, banging it after him and roaring that he's not going to take this crap.

Pat, in fairness, is just trying to rationalize the reasons for our own performance and lack of motivation.

I am stressed. I fuck Pat out of it. We had to play club games before the Waterford game. When else would we play them?

Pat then has a bit of a go at me in front of the players, saying that he has wanted to go hard and I had wanted to go easy. This is true. I'd said it was too early to go too hard, that I thought we'd peaked a month too early in 2005. My argument was that we'd had a tough league campaign and we needed to take it gentle. We've five long months till September.

So I really lose it. I tell him there was only one boss and that is me. We are two men at the end of our tethers.

Pat's being genuine. He's passionate about the team and I knew his intentions are good, he isn't trying to undermine me. I'd be fierce on that, though. There has to be solidarity among management. Or, at worst, the appearance of it.

(I remember a conversation in 2004 on the way to Dublin for the All-Ireland final. We were on the train and I said to Pat that this was it, whatever went wrong now, we had to wear masks. Players couldn't know there was anything wrong. It's always the same. Nothing in front of the players. Ever.)

Meanwhile Sean Walsh, having run out one door shouting that he didn't have to listen to this, has gone around and come back in another door. Seeing Sean come back in is sort of comical.

The four of us – myself, Ger, Johnny and Pat – have a crisis meeting in Johnny's for a couple of hours that evening. Pat apologizes and says he wasn't having a go, it was just the frustration boiling in him. I know. We all feel it.

On Monday I meet Pat one-on-one in my regular spot for these things, the Bianconi in Killorglin. We let it all hang out. A fairly frayed meeting. I'm still tired and cranky and I let it all go.

It's a delicate balance between two friends. He's a sensitive guy, Pat. He takes criticisms personally. I'm different. A fella can fuck me out of it. I'll fuck him out of it. We'll get on with it.

I say again that I just feel that in the year before we hadn't done enough of the stuff we needed to do. I'm thinking that these hoors from Tyrone will wear us down again unless we are hard into the tackling and intensity. I am determined that, whatever happened last year, we have to change tack now.

In training Pat and I had a difference a little while back about some exercise where the players were playing tippy-tappy stuff with the ball. Our relationship is getting tense now. It's showing a bit in me.

Pat rings me the next evening and offers to resign. I say to Pat that if I wanted him to resign I'd ask him to resign. I don't. We agree to kick to touch.

We have five months left to September. I just want to be over all this with Pat. I know he feels that in the middle of all the frustration I am losing faith in him. I'm not. I am just trying to explain to him that if there's something I disagree with in training, I'm going to tell him. That's not the same thing.

We have to have the occasional robust exchange of views. So what about it? We have a cranky few days, but it's good to have it out. Sometimes you have to have the odd blow-up to cleanse the whole relationship.

Training in the week after the Waterford match was good. We were back in Fitzgerald Stadium, which helped. We had a real sense of purpose back, and we got down to trying to kick ball longer and out wide to the half-forwards. We got them one-on-one with their men and put them under pressure to break tackles and do damage.

We'd been running and hand-passing without width in games. Kick more ball into space and have more fellas isolated was the new modification. We were doing maybe too many drills in narrow spaces. That gets into players' heads. We need more width. We'd been playing in heaps up and down the middle. Width, width, width.

Outside in the big bad world, of course the storm clouds are gathering. Mikey Sheehy is scathing in his criticism in *The Kerryman*. It's the manager's fault not to have players tuned in.

Thanks, Mikey.

Owen McCrohan, also in *The Kerryman*, is working a familiar theme. God Be with the Days When Kerry Massacred Teams Like Waterford, etc., etc.

They're coming out and circling in the sky and May isn't even out! We won the league a few weeks ago, by eight points against a Galway team. We beat Waterford by eight points!

I know this is Kerry, and September is all that counts, but a bit of breathing space would be handy.

I know that, whatever about back in South Kerry, my face doesn't fit with the townies in Tralee and Killarney. When the arrows start coming at me from the pass, I know the rocks that the Indians are hiding behind.

I've a good relationship with the Dr Crokes players on the team but had the odd run-in with Pat O'Shea, their manager, when I was running the team out in Coláiste na Sceilge and he was looking after the Kerry minors. Fair enough.

Then a few weeks back, after we'd announced the team for the league final, Pat O'Shea rang me and asked is it okay for Eoin Brosnan to go with Crokes to play an old Kerry league game down in Cahirciveen on the Saturday, the day before the league final? Be good for his confidence, said O'Shea pointedly.

I asked if this was some sort of a wind-up. It wasn't. Well, wouldn't it be great for Eoin's 'confidence', I said, if he came on in the league final and just cut loose?

I was stunned. Asking a county player to play a Kerry league game in Cahirciveen against a weak side when the county team is playing for a national title the following day! I know Pat has to look out for the Crokes, but I need to stand my ground for the county team as well.

I know even now, in June, that this will be a big part of the season. Ferocious heat coming at me from all angles.

Eamon Breen's column in the local paper gives some respite. On the Waterford game Eamon is dead sound. Kerry struggled. Couldn't lift themselves. Move on.

Nail on the head, Eamon.

The sessions improved. We started a lot of speed endurance work. Speed endurance training usually forms the later part of pre-season training. It's tough work. The sprints are longer and the rest intervals are shorter. The idea is to increase the various components of anaerobic power and capacity.

About ten days after the Waterford game we got two fifteens together for a match. Gooch kicked 1–4 off Marc Sé. Paul O'Connor was flying. We tried Bryan Sheehan at fourteen. We learned a lot.

The mantra for the next night was slightly changed again. The half-forwards need the ball higher up the pitch to engage their men. The half-forwards have been coming too far back, looking for ball. Their men are dropping off and covering in front of the full-forward line. We wanted to get the half-forwards making lateral runs across their line instead of coming down towards the man with the ball. Watch the All-Ireland final. Seán O'Sullivan makes a fifty-yard lateral run along the half-forward line. Just loses his man. Gets the ball half turned and ready to go.

Against Tipperary, in the second round of the Munster championship, we improved. We didn't get a lot of credit for improving, but we improved. We had more focus. We scored 0–17 and conceded 1–5. The Gooch, though, didn't score from play for the second championship match in a row. This caught the imagination around the place.

With Kerry confidence (or arrogance) we had arranged a challenge with Galway for the Friday night after the Tipperary game. We were banking on it being a better game for us. Instead it was a disaster.

We went up to the Gaelic Grounds in Limerick and drew 2–16 apiece. That sounds like decent scoring, but the forwards didn't function. The half-forward line was non-existent. Gooch was marked not interested. Paul O'Connor stuck a great goal after coming on as a sub. That would be enough to get him his place for the Munster final.

Suddenly we are seeing ourselves as the newspapers see us. A team with a lot of problems. We're not gelling in attack. We're not believing in ourselves anywhere on the field. We have a Munster final against Cork in nine days' time.

Problems. Tom O'Sullivan has begun the annual Push-The-Manager-As-Far-As-He-Can-Be-Pushed game. Not long after the Tipp match we had another full-scale fifteen-a-side practice match scheduled for the stadium in Killarney. Five minutes before training I heard the familiar old chirp of the mobile phone. Text from Tom O'Sullivan. Can't make it. Working.

I was mad. My fingers were busy with the furious reply almost before I'd finished reading the text. Tap. Tap. Tap.

'What do you suggest, Tom? That I go in corner back myself, is it? We had 30 players picked for tonight. You could have told me yesterday when I could get a replacement. What do you think, Tom?'

No reply comes. The next day I tried to call Tom. No answer. No return call.

It was hurting me now. This is a man who can come out of a defence with his head up, and put the ball about like Beckenbauer or Bobby Moore. But he's not going to kill himself for me. Tom's the sort of a fella who, if he needed 200 points in the Leaving, he might get 201. He wouldn't go and get 250. And I hate people not returning calls.

So once again. Tap, tap, tap. New text.

'Tom, you will regret not returning my call. I want no casual footballers in my squad. If you don't think it worth your while to return my call you can fuck off. J.'

No reply again. No word of Tom O'Sullivan till the next training session. Nothing got said at that. It was in my head then that, come hell or high water, Tom wouldn't be playing against Cork.

When the week of the Cork game came about, we had the luxury of choice. Mike McCarthy was coming back into the team after the broken finger. The management had the chance to go for the jugular, a rare opportunity to make a point to a good player without weakening the team. I called Tom. Told him he was dropped. Lollipopped.

I had his attention now.

'You're dropping me? Against Cork? Cork?'

Tom O'Sullivan is from Rathmore, which is hard on the border with Cork. This is like being excluded from a family wedding for him. He loves playing against Cork.

'Cork?' he said again. 'You're dropping me against Cork. Cork? You could drop me against anyone, but not Cork. C'mon!'

I'd hit a nerve. Tom is a smooth operator. That was the first time in three years that he'd shown sign of a temper. Again the old lesson had served me well. Wait and pick your battle.

After that night I knew Tom was as sore as a bear with me. You expect that from players who are dropped, and in the circumstances there was always going to be a little bad feeling. I didn't expect what greeted me the next night at training.

I arrived down, got out of the car and spotted Tom's brother Dan, hanging around the place. He was just inside the gate, right near the dressing room.

I spotted him before he spotted me so I put the head down and I kept going. Got into the dressing room, sat down. I'm not going out near him in case he hits me a clip in front of the players.

I put the gear on and go out with a gang of the boys. We go past Dan O'Sullivan again. He gives me a nod.

'What the fuck is Tom O'Sullivan's brother doing here?' I asked the lads as we hit the pitch.

They'd no idea.

Fuck.

I'm out on the field now and almost afraid to go back into the dressing room. There's criticism, and there's heat . . . and there's this. They're a sticky crowd out in Rathmore. Tom's gone and organized the brother and Aidan O'Mahony to give me a pasting. These fuckers are going to gang up and beat me.

I see Harry O'Neill the masseur come out. He shakes Dan's hand. Calls over to me.

'Jack. Should have said. Have Dan in to help out with the massages this week. Getting busy coming to the final.'

I just nod.

'Okay, Harry. How's it goin', Dan?'

Jesus.

13

Home again. We opened the pub with a bang and I got involved in the football straight away. While I was away Dromid Pearses had gone nowhere. They were still a gang of social footballers, playing novice championship and Division Five League. Part of me said that I'd best know where my bread is buttered here. No hope for a publican in Dromid if he plays football for Waterville. Part of me was filled with ambition, too. I still had a dream that Dromid could be a serious place to play football. Often on the scaffolding in Manhattan I'd have found myself daydreaming about what Dromid could do with a decent team.

So I went back and threw the hand in with the boys in Dromid. I was near enough straight back into training them when I got off the plane in 1989. I remember the first time I saw them out on the field after I had come home. The pub had set things going quickly, fellas talking and daydreaming. I remember going out to training and there was twenty-six or twenty-seven out. Not a bad start to have such a great buzz in the parish. The Tavern meant that there was a centre for the first time. That was the old daydream coming back, to make a community and a team. It would all take off from there, we hoped.

It did. The community began to develop. In terms of meeting people, the bar made a huge impact to our remote rural area. Before there was Mass on a Sunday and then home. The bar gave people a chance to be something else. Friends and neighbours. And the whole area took a little bit of self-respect out of it. It's hard to put a finger on, but it just gave everyone a little lift to have a focal point for the community and the club.

Football changed. There used to be just a pitch and a dressing room. When the Tavern opened, there'd be sandwiches after a game. Everyone would mingle. The opposing team would come back too, and they'd leave in the evening with a different impression of Dromid. Not just a gang of wild mountain men.

When people got a bit of pride in the place, other initiatives started. There was a community centre built, some factory units, a hostel, and places for old people. There used to be just a primary school and a few houses. It all came because of a pub and a football team.

Soon after I came back I was training three teams: the club, the school team and Kerry techs. I was behind the bar the rest of the time, cajoling fellas to get involved and telling the social drinkers on the team that I was keeping an eye on them. All the old enthusiasm and obsession came back straight away when I hit home.

My attitude was better this time, but I still had my moments. I couldn't take no for an answer from any fella and was still inclined to be a bit confrontational and argumentative. If a fella didn't do what I told him, I still couldn't hack it. I was cranky on the pitch, and if players weren't doing what I wanted them to do I'd fuck them out of it. Not great for the local publican to be doing.

We were average as a team, just ploughing away. We had a good player called Dan Fitzpatrick. He played Kerry junior, maybe Under-21 too. Of course I had rows with him and he skedaddled off to Waterville.

We'd a big fella called Crusher Daly, and I remember one night getting into an argument with Crusher. He was flaking me off the ball with his big paws. I told him to fuck off. He had two hands on him like shovels and he took a couple of steps towards me. I took four or five steps backwards. This was an animal of a man. If he caught me, he'd kill me.

A few years later, in the run-up to a match against Waterville, I got into another row down on the field and this time I didn't step back quick enough. I got my jaw broken. I didn't ask the club to back me this time. Relations with Waterville had sunk to an all-time low, and we hated them so much nobody wanted to miss the game on Sunday. I turned up late with my broken jaw and played. It made the point. The man that broke it drifted off this time.

I started back with the club in the winter of 1989, and the following spring we reached the final of a Gaeltacht tournament back in Gallarus, near Páidí Ó Sé's place. We had a massive weekend up there. We got to the final and we were nine points up with ten minutes to go against the locals from CorcaDhuibhne. They came back and drew with us and then beat us in extra time. They had a couple of fellas playing who we found out afterwards were of dodgy origin for a Gaeltacht tournament. I remember Micheál Ó Sé commentating in Irish. On the pitch I could hear him getting excited on the sideline. 'There'll be bonfires around the Inny Tavern tonight. *Beidh tinte cnáimh timpeall Tabhairne na h-Ine anocht! Oh cúl. Cúl eile.*'

That was my first encounter with Páidí. He was running the bar and taking the cash in, hand over fist. There was money going over that counter in a blizzard. I think that's where Páidí got the notion for his own *comórtas*.

We soldiered on. In 1991 we won a novice championship. Times were still hard and, great occasion as that day was, a few of the team had to leave straight away for work back in London the next day.

Slowly we were learning to win. In Dromid we will always remember a famous game against St Michael's, Ballinskelligs, in 1992. We were ten points down at half-time and we went down another point again at the beginning of the second half. We came back to draw, and we beat them in the replay. That was the qualifying game from South Kerry to go to Donegal for that year's Gaeltacht tournament.

And when we look back over all that's happened for Dromid, we always stop at that Gaeltacht tournament in 1992 in Gweedore, which is about as far north in this country as you can go. Still, it was no hardship. Jeremiah Shea and Mike Sé in the club remember putting an entire team into two cars and driving to a previous Gaeltacht tournament in Donegal. Two car-loads going the length of the country to Donegal, and John Sheehan made his way from Dublin. Dromid were beaten in the quarter-final by a point that time, and it remained our ambition to win the Gaeltacht tournament.

Anyway, we went up to Donegal with no great hope and carrying a few imports who could no more speak a sentence in Irish than I could speak one in Mandarin.

For the Gaeltacht weekend, you have to speak Irish throughout the games. Toorsaleen is supposedly a Gaeltacht, but most lads have only pidgin Irish. I wasn't too bad, and in the run-up I'd be teaching the Irish as well as the tactics. The vocabulary of the other lads was pretty limited. '*Maith Thú* Crusher!'

Of course, when we got up there, in the first tense match it was me who forgot the rules. I let some spiel out of me in English at one of the lads, and the referee came to book me.

'*Cád is ainm duit?*'

'*Sean Ó Conchubair.*'

Ten minutes later he struck on me again for the same thing.

'*Cád is ainm duit?*'

I looked at him. Chanced it.

'*Sean Ó Sé?*'

I got away with it and stayed on the pitch.

In the semi-final we had a bit of a setback. The local curate, Father Gerry Keane, was playing for us. He was taken out of it with a high challenge and the Order of Malta carried him away. They took him to hospital in Letterkenny. It was Sunday afternoon. Our poor hard-working chairman, Jeremiah Shea, had to go off to collect him late at night. He picked up the priest with the jersey still on him. Jeremiah helped get him ready. He drank a pint or two to revive himself and lined out the next day at full-forward. He rattled in the first goal against the locals, and often the song was sung in the Inny Tavern afterwards,

> '*Who put the ball in the Gweedore net?*
> *The curate did*'

After the semi-final was won in extra time, word got back to the Inny Tavern in Dromid. There was great talk and great excitement and many drinks to the team. So many drinks that at midnight it was decided for many of the congregation that missing the final the next day would be a sin.

So fifteen mad men decided at midnight to hire a minibus there and then and head for Gweedore on the pilgrimage of all pilgrimages. They set out on the most epic voyage since Shackleton's trek, leaving the Inny Tavern at one in the morning with steam coming out their ears from the drink. They took a few stools from the bar and put them in the centre aisle for extra accommodation. They took some bottles of whiskey to keep them going and an accordion in case there was any danger of sleep.

And off they went, drinking and singing through the night, right up the length of Ireland.

They hit Gweedore at nine in the morning and they were like fifteen walking ghosts coming out of the bus. My brother Joe was among them. Humphrey Boola, Mickey Tir na hAilte, Seaneen Caslagh, the whole gang of them. There was nothing for it, the way they looked, than to get into a pub and put a few pints into themselves and get some life back.

We won the match in extra time, our fourth tough match of the weekend. We had a good young fella in Dromid at the time, Kieran Bobby O'Sullivan. He played with the Kerry minors and we had fierce trouble getting him released for the weekend. He was our star, and our main tactic was getting him the ball.

Kieran Bobby was overshadowed in the end, though, by an unlikely figure. Late in extra time Gweedore came at us. They had a boy off the Donegal Under-21 side and he had some pace. Suddenly he was bursting straight towards our goal and looking fresh as a daisy. Crusher Daly, not the fastest man on earth, cut behind him at some point and, realizing he wasn't going to catch him for a textbook tackle, jumped on his back like a stout tiger bringing down a gazelle. They missed the free in. Crusher's foul was so unbelievable that he got away with a telling-off.

The minibus gang was still alive and well. Humphrey Boola had that accordion. After the cup was handed over, he played in the middle of the field and they danced a set there in the park in Gweedore.

It was mad and it was unbelievable. It epitomized the spirit in Dromid.

You wonder if it's an exaggeration to say that a pub and a football team built the community. Well, the Udarás na Gaeltachta people who were in Gweedore had never seen such scenes. Set-dancing after a Gaelic football match where everyone spoke Irish. Every grant that we looked for in Dromid and a few we didn't look for came our way in the next few years.

For me, the pace of living in Dromid grew surprisingly Manhattan-like. I began to wonder where was the quality of life I had come home for. My old headmaster, Con Dineen, a great man and a huge influence on my life, had persuaded me to begin teaching again. So I was teaching in my old school, Scoil Uí Chonaill.

It was such a pleasure to work with Con. He would take me off to play golf on the odd Friday afternoon, just the two of us slipping away to play a few holes. As a man-manager Con was a genius and I learned more from him maybe than from anyone else. Taking me away like that on Fridays made me feel special. I felt like an important man having a clandestine arrangement with the headmaster. I'd have run up Carrantouhill three times a day for Con if he'd have asked me to.

So I was tending bar, teaching kids and training three teams. Bridie was rearing the kids on her own. Something had to give.

It couldn't be the football. It couldn't be the teaching. So, after a few years of everything being so hectic, I got sense and decided to sell out of the bar. Mike bought my holding and I focused on teaching and football. The bar had brought me home from America, but selling my share of it gave me the life I had been hoping for.

I'd always dreamed of having my own haven in Kerry to escape to. We were driving to Bridie's parents' house near St Finan's Bay one day, and I was gazing at the beach and the scenery and thinking that it would be some spot to build a house on. Views of Puffin Island and the Skelligs.

There was a farmer's field down there and on impulse I asked the owner, Mike Connell, would he sell us the field. He said he would. I went back and hit him for another bit. And we built a house facing the Atlantic. On bad days the spray from the foam hits our front window, and on good days the boys surf as we watch from the sitting room.

In the club we had good young players coming through the under-age ranks. The one that caught my eye was a kid called Declan O'Sullivan. He was a distant relative of mine on my mother's side. Declan's mother was a Sheehan from Coombaha, which is just on the other shoulder of the mountain my mother grew up on.

As a young fella Declan had all the signs that he'd be a footballer. I watched him winning championships from Under-12 on. He had that swerve and that way of carrying himself that marks a good footballer out. And he was keen. Mad for road.

On Sundays, after Mass in the church, I'd keep an eye out for his family car and knock on the window and tell them to let Declan out. We'd go down to the new field (the club got its present pitch opened in 1991) and we'd kick for an hour or two before I'd drop him to the family house, out towards Waterville direction.

Declan went on to make his senior debut for the club when he was just fifteen years old. We were playing St Michael's of Foilmore and we were a couple short. Somebody threw him a bag of gear and he was on for the second half. Players who have a bit of greatness in them always make a mark early on. Declan had the confidence, the bit of a sidestep and swerve, and he had physique. He scored a goal for us.

By then he had graduated from John Bosco's to be a pupil of mine in Coláiste na Sceilge. The next few years would be special. They would change our lives, and when they were over I would find myself sitting in the car looking out at the school field in Cahirsciveen in the early hours of the morning with tears running down my face.

PART THREE

Summer

14

9 July 2006. Kerry 0–10, Cork 0–10.

This is the day summer begins. And what a day. Cork seven points to Kerry's one point with five minutes to half-time. Fierce aggression by Cork. Fierce. Morgan throwing a water bottle when a decision went against him. Lynch gets sent off before half-time. We peg them back to 0–7 0–4. They kick two at the start of the second half, but we reel them in gradually. Sheehan misses a couple of frees he would normally get. Gooch misses a thirty-yarder. Sheehan kicks two points from play and we go one up. Can't pull away, though. Cork dominate the last few minutes. Masters kicks a shot. One umpire signals wide, the other a point. Pandemonium breaks out. Ref overrules the umpire and we get out of jail. Jim Carney interviews me coming off the field. I shoot him a dirty look when he says the point was disallowed for a square ball or a bad hand-pass. I tell him that it was obvious from the body language of the players that it was wide. Somebody says into his earpiece that it was a square ball. Michael Lyster back in the studio says I look bewildered. Spot on, Michael. Bewildered. And bothered.

Jesus. Morgan had been giving out his old standard tune all year about us being cynical and I never really sussed it. I know now why he enjoys that one so much. Cork came down to Killarney and they were all business. They burst out from the dressing-room corner of the field and immediately hunted us out of our traditional Kerry dugout. They told us in very certain terms to shag away off up to the other dugout.

Morgan knew what he was doing. He has an obsession with Kerry and he's been thinking about this for a long time. He knows you're souped up for the day of a Munster final. Even the small things, the *piseogs*, the traditions matter. Familiarity brings you a bit of reassurance. That's why fellas sit in the same place. You sit beside a new fella, you're not used to his *geatsaís* or routine, and it distracts you.

The smallest things matter in big games. A fella talking out of place in the dressing room. An official coming in and doing something odd. A fella nervous in the coach. Any disruption. You go out on the pitch and you're not in your own dugout and it gets inside your head. I'd have my own patch of the Killarney dugout, my own corner just outside Johnny and Ger. Supporters tend to congregate in the same areas. You'd see an old familiar face behind you when you turn around. You'd hear the same voices. You'd be used to watching a match from there, just like the supporters are. Suddenly I'm up in some other place.

From the word go in Killarney, Cork put us out of kilter. That was the plan. Pressure at every point.

Morgan raved like a lunatic all day, contested every decision. Kept the pressure up. At one stage there was an incident on the sideline. I sauntered up to see what was going on. A Cork selector threatened to bate me up to the stand if I didn't go away. Poor Paul O'Connor from Kenmare got the roughest debut of his life. An off-the-ball elbow flaked at his ear left his head ringing for fifteen minutes. I saw who did it, too. They were flaking us at all angles.

Fuck. Morgan has known all year what he was doing. He was hoping that with all his talk since February about us being cynical we'd be watching ourselves in front of the referee.

Cork came tearing into us. More aggressive, hungrier. Stronger. I'm wondering as I'm watching all this, Jesus, why are we not at this level of intensity too – are we not right?

The game is sort of a blur. We need to move Aidan O'Mahony out to wing-back fairly early on, so Tom O'Sullivan gets a reprieve and gets shoved into the corner. Mossy Lyons is the one who loses out. I feel guilty about that.

Mossy played in all the league games, did nothing out of the way. He played the league final, first round of championship, second round, and he's started the Munster final since Tom was dropped to put manners on him. After twenty minutes though,

My parents on their wedding day,
9 January 1951.

My father and I on our farm in Dromid.

In the meadow: my brother Tim is in front; just behind are my brothers Pat and
Joe, my mother, and my sisters Sheila and Mary; in back are my brother Mike, my
grandmother, sister Joan, my father with me on his lap, and my grandfather.

A New York wedding: with Bridie in Upper Manhattan on our big day.

The Inny Tavern, which my brother Mike and I built, became a great focus for the community in Dromid.

Working as a Kerry selector under Páidí Ó Sé was always an adventure. Here he's having a polite word with Pat McEnaney after Tomás got sent off in the 2001 quarter-final against Dublin. (*Domnick Walsh/Eye Focus*)

Jer O'Shea congratulating Kieran Cronin on his goal for Coláiste na Sceilge in the 2002 Colleges Senior. A semi-final replay against St Jarlath's of Tuam. After the heartbreaking loss, Jer gave a brilliant speech about the team that had us in tears. His death the following summer, at the age of twenty, was a devastating blow for all of us.

(*Damien Eagers/Sportsfile*)

Ecstasy at the final whistle of our All-Ireland victory over Mayo in 2004: Sean Walsh, chairman of the county board, takes up the chase.

One year later, coming home to Tralee after the final, it's a different story: you can tell from the looks on our faces – Sean, Colm Cooper, Jer O'Keeffe and I – that we've lost to Tyrone. (*Domnick Walsh/Eye Focus*)

Losing to Cork in the 2006 Munster final replay may have been the best thing that ever happened to us, but shaking hands with Billy Morgan afterwards was not my happiest moment. (*Brendan Moran/Sportsfile*)

We got our revenge in the All-Ireland semi-final. Here I am celebrating with Kieran Donaghy, whose move to full-forward was one of the things that turned our season around.

Restoring Declan O'Sullivan to the team – and therefore to the captaincy – for the 2006 All-Ireland final was a controversial decision, because it meant Colm Cooper lost his chance to lift the cup as captain. Except he didn't lose his chance: Declan and Gooch lifted the cup together. (*Brendan Moran/Sportsfile*)

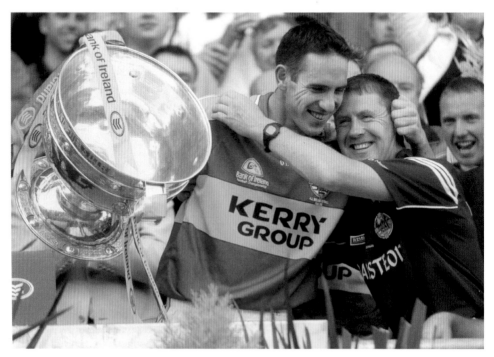

Declan and I had achieved our dream, and we would be bringing the cup back to our home place in Dromid. (*Brendan Moran/Sportsfile*)

In Dromid with Sam and my father: the sweetest homecoming.

In the Bridge Bar, getting sustenance while on tour of the national schools in South Kerry with the cup.

At home in St Finan's Bay with Bridie and our sons Eanna (*left*) and Cian (*photo: Michael Brosnan*), and (*below*) with the cup.

when there was nothing happening, we've had to sacrifice Mossy. He's done nothing wrong, we're just looking for something different. Seamus is back. Mike Mac is back, and finally the squeeze has come. Mossy is going to feel hard done by, and if he doesn't get back in he'll look at the league and the opening championship games and think we were just putting him in for the spin, so that we could put a bit of *cur isteach* into some of the other fellas. A fella doesn't have to come to you when he feels that way. You can see it in his body language.

Anthony Lynch throws a poke at Kieran Donaghy and gets sent off. At half-time, we're in trouble even though we're a man up. We don't have the intensity they have. Nowhere near.

Once in 2004, against Limerick, we had the backs to the wall as well. I laid it on the line. Told them they were playing for their futures in the Kerry jersey. I had three years; they only had 35 minutes. That's the sort of card a manager plays only once. It's a first-year management trick.

This time, we are all in it together. I warned them after Lynch got sent off that the referee would try to even things up. Told them to watch for it.

Hey presto! Towards the end of the game I see Kieran Donaghy walking out towards me on the sideline.

'Hey, Donaghy! Where you going?'

'I got sent off.'

'What did you do?'

'Nothing.'

'Nothing?'

'I swear to you. Nothing.'

Then it's over. A draw. I've hardly had a moment to draw breath.

Next evening we meet as a team.

The meeting is under a different format from usual, and it goes well. We have been dead all season. We won the league without pushing too hard. We accounted for the poor Waterford and Tipperary performances by saying we were in a lull after the league. But we're not pulling out. The edge isn't there. We may not be in the comfort zone, but we're not anywhere we want to be. So we divide the players into groups and we set them the task of talking about where the players want to be and what they think is wrong.

Pat and Ger have organized this well. The groups are well chosen. Enough leaders and enough young players in each. They can say what they like in their responses. We're in the last-chance saloon and we'll listen to anything.

Group 1: Seamus Moynihan, Seán O'Sullivan, Tommy Griffin, Paul O'Connor, Kieran Donaghy and Tomás Ó Sé.

They come back with a lot of tactical points. No support coming out of defence. Look for outlet passes. There's a few small things added at the end that are interesting and show how the guys are thinking.

- No mobiles etc. before game.
- Move warm-up closer to game.
- Rumours of hassle in camp abound but are untrue.

This last point is killing us. According to the rumours, we are running a madhouse. Certain players won't play with certain others. Declan has hit some bad form and, according to rumours, I'm being told by the west Kerry players to drop him or they walk. Where is this stuff coming from?

Group 2: Mike McCarthy, Killian Young, Darren O'Sullivan, Aidan O'Mahony, Bryan Sheehan, Aodán MacGearailt, Ronan Hussey.

Again tactics. And a request for more one-on-ones in training with forwards become backs also.

Group 3: Paul Galvin, Declan O'Sullivan, Padraig Reidy, Kieran O'Leary, Brendan Guiney, Diarmuid Murphy.

This is the most interesting group:

- Many in group not being heard.
- Something missing in squad. Spirit? Atmosphere?
- Not fighting for each other, not supporting.

- Suggestion for mentors. One to one for younger players matched with more experienced players, advise and support progress.
- All wary of each other, looking after themselves. Need to pull together.
- Need for more liaison with county board . . . improve support structures.
- Need to agree and all abide by team rules, events, etc.

This is Declan's group. In a forward line that just isn't working he's struggling with his form. I think part of it might be burnout, and I have a mind to take some of the captaincy responsibilities off Declan. I'm sure the idea of liaison with the county board has come from him. He takes too much on his shoulders when he needs to just worry about the football pure and simple. It's killing him. He's worrying about gear, logistics. Peripheral stuff. Let him go back and play ball. There are a lot of other solid guys who can take some of that load up for him.

Group 4: Eoin Brosnan, Darragh Ó Sé, Mossy Lyons, Marc Ó Sé, Colm Cooper, Mike Frank Russell.

More older players in this group, but some interesting points. A lot of tactical aspirations. More turnovers! Apply training to games! A moan: Training Too Hard and Too Long on Tuesday! And again some talk about team ethic. Eat together, travel together, team ethic needed, not personal gain.

Small things add up: wear team gear, super attitude in training needs to be carried outside sessions.

We're pleased with what the players have come up with, and the talk that follows is useful. I'm glad that the issue of the cliques is out in the open. There is a clique around the Ó Sé's which I think intimidates other guys on the team. Not intentionally. It's just, when you have three brothers who are so close and so good, and you then add in the few friends, you end up with a cluster of strong personalities. They form the hub of the team and I think a lot of the other players think that they just revolve around them.

We talk afterwards about players not playing a team game on or off the pitch. Is there a problem of passing the ball to selective people in training? Do people feel intimidated? We need to do everything together. The phrase we use is 'ferocious togetherness'. That involves subs not sulking. Players not bitching. I hope this is the spark we need. Cork have put it up to us as a team. The players have put it up to us as a management.

If we don't respond there's something wrong with us.

We talk finally about the wild stories doing the rounds about rifts in the camp. Darragh Ó Sé is supposed to have hit me a skelp one evening in a row about picking Declan. How can you deal with bullshit like that? Come out as Kerry manager and say that no, Darragh Ó Sé hasn't been beating me?

There's cliques, but the lies going around don't even have that right. At the meeting, talking and laughing about it brings the players closer together.

We're going training again on Thursday night and we've decided this time it will be behind closed doors. They can't tell lies about us if they can't see us. This will work out!

The reaction in print and in the saloon bars to the locked-door training session is that it is a 'new low' in Kerry football. It seems that this is the first time ever a Kerry team has trained behind closed doors. Soon people are ringing me with the latest rumours. There's been so many rows and walkouts that I ordered the doors shut to keep discontented players from leaving during training.

They really do believe outside that we're running a madhouse here.

15

Here's a story now. If you go over the mountain from my house in St Finan's Bay and down through Portmagee you'll find yourself at the bridge connecting Valentia Island to the rest of the country. There's a spot on Valentia Island called Paris and there's a famous character from Paris called Michael Murphy.

In The Bridge Bar in Portmagee they refer to Michael Murphy as 'Murphy Paris' (pronounced the French way as Murphy Paree). Murphy Paris is typical of the passionate breed that follows South Kerry football.

Murphy Paris has two passions in life. Kerry football, especially South Kerry football and Maurice Fitzgerald. And beagling. He esteems his beagle, Rover, above most human beings.

Back in 2000, when I'd rowed in behind Páidí Ó Sé again, the controversy of the summer was about South Kerry and Maurice Fitzgerald. It works like politics. As a selector from South Kerry my job was to be in there, defending Maurice Fitzgerald to the death. The local selector has to pull for the local man. Nowhere more than here in this part of the county where we feel we don't get a fair shake at the best of times.

After one of the Armagh games that season (the first one, I think), I took refuge with a pint in The Bridge Bar in Portmagee. Sometimes when you need a bit of peace in out of the elements, there's nothing better than to find a corner in The Bridge with a pint and paper to hide behind.

It was a Tuesday evening and I was settled into my spot with the paper unfolded when I heard Murphy Paris coming in for the last stop before home in the long journey back from Croke Park. He was in good fettle.

Naturally he spots me. Naturally he comes over.

He's on about the football, of course. Maurice Fitz. The Man with the Golden Legs.

'Why aren't ye starting Maurice Fitz?' he says straight up.

We get into it for a minute or two. Me defending myself. Murphy Paris not accepting any explanation at all.

A big gang gathers around for the banter. They know the form of Murphy Paris and they know the form of myself.

I don't want to have the argument. I've enough of it for the moment.

'Murphy,' I says, 'I tell you what you'll do now. Go away and you stick to the beagles. Leave the football to me and you stick to the hunting.'

'You know that's what I'll do, Jack,' he says, turning to go, 'but when I go hunting next Sunday I won't leave Rover in the boot of the car.'

And off he goes. Murphy Paris 1, Jack O'Connor 0.*

That's how it is in South Kerry. There's not a lot to shout about and we don't have great confidence in ourselves. If we're going to be as good as the rest, we have to know we are better. The great South Kerry footballers have that about them. A bit of style and a need to prove something.

The GAA is a group of tribes. We like to think that the county is a tribe but it's much more parochial than that. At the end of the day, people have their own pride in their spot, their own reasons in their own heart.

We only have a divisional team to represent us in the county championship and we've never got to see a club side from here go

---

*There's a little sequel to that one, which became famous in The Bridge Bar. The following year, 2001, Murphy Paris was in Croke Park to see Kerry being beaten by Meath. Beaten out the gate, as it happened. Maurice Fitz was brought on that day to do the fire-brigade job before half-time, but there was no hope.

Somebody met Murphy Paris a couple of days later. Rather than discussing the match at all, Paris says mournfully, 'Do you know we were never worse. And as for poor old Rover, when he got the run he never even wagged his tail.'

to Croke Park on All-Ireland Final day. All that is part of the reason why the Coláiste na Sceilge team that Declan O'Sullivan grew up on took such a hold on the imagination.

There was a unique bond there. Two bonds, in fact. One between ourselves as a team, and another between the team and the South Kerry public. The adventure represents two years of our lives together and a time when the whole of South Kerry fell in love with a school football team.

At the turn of the millennium we'd gone into this new amalgamated school in Cahirciveen. As a staff we were attempting to mould three different schools – a convent and two vocational schools – into one community. It was going to be difficult. Just as football made a community of us out in Dromid, it did the same in Coláiste na Sceilge. The bit of success we enjoyed was manna from heaven.

In Scoil Uí Chonaill, where I'd been a pupil and where I'd taught, we were in the vocational sector up to then. We won the All-Ireland Vocational Schools title in 1997, we had a school population of 140, including girls. The local Christian Brothers had closed a few years previously and we got all their good footballers! We beat St Malachy's of Castlewellan in that final. St Malachy's had 700–800 kids to choose from, so it was a huge win for us as underdogs.

That was the start. We won the competition again two years later, but we'd joined up with Waterville to become Cahirciveen Post-Primary by then. We came through in a great final in Portlaoise that year. We beat Cookstown from Tyrone. A fella called Peter Canavan was training them and they had a big kid by the name of Owen Mulligan in the middle of the field. Mulligan kicked three points.

Then the following year, 2000, the new school had come together. Coláiste na Sceilge. We won the Vocational Schools All-Ireland again. We beat a crowd from Mayo. Alan Dillon was playing for them. Gary Dillon was playing, too. So teams from Cahirciveen had won the Vocational Schools title three times under different names in the space of a few years.

Winning Vocational Schools All-Irelands would, you'd think, be good enough for a small isolated area like ours, but there's the old insecurity about everything we achieve here. In South Kerry, people never want to talk up a good young player. In the towns like Tralee and Killarney, they talk fellas up all the time. They'll write about them in the local papers. Next big thing! Here, we keep people in their place. I wonder sometimes where would a young fella get his confidence from. You hear the comments. He's good, but he's not strong enough. He's fast enough, but sure he's not brave. He's not the distant relation of a footballer.

We decided after that third win in 2000 to do something bold and something a bit out of character. We entered ourselves into the Colleges competition rather than continuing in the Vocational Schools competition. It was a gamble. We knew we'd be looked down on by the big traditional powers. We knew that if we failed badly we'd be laughed at, not just by the old schools who dominate the competition but by people in South Kerry. We were doing something a bit uppity.

The Munster schools competition is the Corn Uí Mhuirí. Get through that and you play in the Hogan Cup, the holy grail of schools football. As it was, we would win three Corn Uí Mhuirí in a row. Straight out the gate. Nobody beat us for three straight years.

In that time the team unified a new school and captured the imagination of the whole of South Kerry. We got big crowds, tons of newspaper coverage. People rang in to national radio programmes and told the nation that this was a great team and that these were some great games. I remember Ger O'Keeffe, who I didn't know well at the time, talking to Des Cahill about one of our games he had seen.

It was a special time. I can get misty-eyed just talking about it. The boys were very close, a band of brothers. They'd grown up together, and part of their personality as a group was to be seen in the style of football they played. It's rare to see such flowing, combined football from a young team. It was a joy to behold; and the style, the enthusiasm, it all came from them, their closeness and the people they were.

As a group they'd have done anything for each other. It seemed almost natural to them that they had such good movement off the ball, fellas backing each other up all the way. We were blessed with two great wing-backs, two fine midfielders and the kind of full-forward line that any coach dreams about. Declan O'Sullivan was full-forward. He was a prodigy then, a machine for scoring and the captain and the leader of the team. On either side of him he had two natural-born corner-forwards, Joe Corridan of Derrynane and Jer O'Shea of Foilmore. Behind them they had a wonderful workhorse of a half-forward, Kieran Cronin. Perfect balance.

In that forward line Declan could do anything, and the two lads outside him could read whatever he would do. Jer O'Shea had a trigger-happy left foot and the brain to go with it. Nothing ever on Jer's mind but to score points. Joe Corridan on the other side was a dynamo.

That first year the pitch, which now lies at the back of the school, was still seeding and it lay unfinished. So we trained on a narrow strip the length of the pitch and about fifty yards wide. In a way, it was the confines of the training ground that made the boys the team they were. They became very fluent with the ball. It was almost one-touch stuff. A defender could come out of any corner with a tackle in training, so they knew that if they dwelled on the ball they were in trouble. They developed the old Liverpool thing of pass and move. When success came we played a lot of matches in Fitzgerald Stadium, and when we got in there it was like a thousand acres of prairie.

When we upgraded to the Colleges competition, we were behind the eight-ball. New territory.

We wanted to prove everyone wrong. The boys bought into it. If I'd told them to jump in the sea and swim out around the Skelligs and back, they'd have done it.

That first year we became Munster champions when we beat

Killorglin in the Corn Uí Mhuirí final. Each of the full-forward line chipped in with a couple of points. Near the end that day we scored a goal which was typical of the way we played football. Joe Corridan made a run to win a ball out wide. Immediately he gave a clever pass to Jer O'Shea, who had already read what Joe was going to do. Jer just flicked the ball into the path of Sean Courtney, our left wing-forward. Sean didn't catch it but flicked it to the net. If any senior inter-county team scored a goal like that, they'd be replaying it on *The Sunday Game* for months.

We rolled on to the All-Ireland semi-final against the mighty St Pat's of Navan, who were the All-Ireland champions at the time. The game was played on April Fools' Day. We got mugged.

With ten minutes to go we went two points ahead, and after a struggle in the first half everything was working well. Declan O'Sullivan and Jer O'Shea were playing beautifully in the full-forward line and it looked as if the game was over when Declan leaped and flicked a high ball to the Navan net. Both of the umpires pointed for a goal, but the referee, who was a long way from the action, signalled a square ball and disallowed the goal.

A minute before that he had disallowed a point which Declan kicked because it hadn't been from the precise spot that the free had been awarded. And in the first half he had taken another goal back off Declan and awarded a penalty from which we only managed a point.

All bad, but worse was to come. Jer O'Shea kicked a wonderful point to put us three points up with eight minutes left. When there is only a score between two sides, you count the seconds on the sideline. With five minutes left, Navan got a goal through Joe Sheridan. Even back then, Sheridan was shaping as a decent footballer. That goal made it level.

And then two minutes later a big high ball came in on top of our full-back, and Navan's big midfielder, a fella called Darren O'Toole, flicked the ball to the net. It was identical almost to the goal which Declan had seen disallowed a few minutes earlier. This time, though, the goal was awarded.

We fought back. There was no quit in those kids. We got a

point. We kept fighting. We got a little glimpse of salvation when Joe Corridan burst through, right at the end. But his shot at goal was blocked down and that was it. Over.

It was a kick in the guts. Colm O'Rourke, who was the St Pat's coach, was very decent to us. Colm spoke to the boys, he said that sometimes the better team doesn't win, that sometimes you just get away with it. He said he'd have been happy to have snatched a draw, but that was life. If you kept playing football, all those things would even out.

They didn't, though. For that team things never evened out.

16

We have just a week to prepare for the replay against Cork. The pressure is mounting. There's a sense around Kerry that this team and its manager are dead in the water.

On the Friday of the replay weekend, Ger O'Keeffe is in Dublin Airport coming through for work when he spots some familiar faces: an entourage of Corkmen, striding purposefully through the airport in their suits. They head towards the exit signs. Ger knows that they know something. They haven't gone up for a Friday night out in Temple Bar on the weekend of a Munster final. Ger calls me. I call Sean Walsh.

'Sean, they're going to get Anthony Lynch off.'

'Sure they can't do that.'

'They will.'

'Is there anything we can do for Donaghy? This will look bad.'

'It would have to be very last minute.'

I call Donaghy, offer him just a fragment of hope. Next morning there's a text on my phone.

'Jack, can't really sleep. Make sure you try with that appeal again in the morning. Please. I won't let you down if I get on that pitch. Thanks again. Talk tomorrow. Kieran.'

The text was sent at 12.58 a.m. Typical of Donaghy's enthusiasm. In the week after the drawn game his eye was badly swollen. I know he was more sinned against than sinning.

Cork pull the stroke, though. They get Anthony Lynch free. Donaghy takes his punishment. Fair enough, but I have a feeling the karma will come back and bite them.

Not yet, though. Cork 1–12, Kerry 0–9.

We shot fifteen wides. Gooch kicked seven of those himself. It's a long time since he did that in a game, if he ever did. We played much better overall, but still nothing happened up front. Four forwards were taken off, including Declan. Something incredible happened as he came off. The Kerry fans booed him as he came to the dugout. The Kerry captain booed by his own. That genuinely is a new low.

The dressing rooms in Páirc Uí Chaoimh are small, and for some reason you can only get to them by coming through the main spectator access tunnel under the main stand. We flee into them as soon as the final whistle goes. Some of us get in quickly. Others of us are held up by the traffic of fans.

I've got one thing on my mind: I need to get a hold of the players before the bastards who booed us above in that stand get a hold of them. If I don't get them, well, by Tuesday their heads will be poisoned.

We're right at the edge now and, unless we stick together for a few hours through tonight, we are finished. If we walk out the door and into the sunshine and go our separate ways, we are history. Everything that is believed about this team on the outside will be true next time we meet. The loss will have split us up.

I come into the dressing room and I'm one of the last in. I tell Pat the Bag Tatler to mind the door and not to let any players leave. I hit the showers for a quick wash and a think.

When I come back out to talk to the players, the three Ó Sé's are gone. Pat the Bag shrugs. Fuck. Everything I want to say about sticking together flies out the window.

I've got the chairman to call the Hayfield Manor Hotel, where we had a team meeting this morning, and ask, is the room free again. The idea was to go straight back and thrash all this out. Now it's going to be pointless. I say a few words about togetherness anyway, and we head out for the bus. I have no clue where we're going now.

To my surprise the three Ó Sé boys are sitting out there on the bus. The first piece of good news in a week. Shakespeare comes into my head. 'There is a tide in the affairs of men, which, taken at the flood, leads on to fortune . . .'

I should have known. It's not in the character of the west Kerry *fear laidir* to sit around in a dressing room and explain to thirty journalists what he's thinking when Kerry have just lost a Munster final to Cork. They got dressed and got out of there because they hate losing and they hate being in a losing dressing room.

More good news as the bus chugs towards the Hayfield Manor. The draw is made for the qualifiers. We have Longford at home. Longford up in Pearse Park I would genuinely have been worried about. Longford at home, though, seems like the perfect rehabilitation. A game we should win and a chance for the Kerry public to come out and be supportive again. As if we wanted extra incentive, the winners will have to play Armagh. My buddy Jerry Mahony shoots me a text telling me to keep my head up.

A couple of things are going through my head as we drive: Sticking together . . . ferocious togetherness. And one other thing. Somebody in the camp or near to it is spinning yarns to journalists. Bullshit stories. When we get into the room in the Hayfield Manor, it's almost the first thing I roar out of me. Everything is still set up from our morning meeting and the lads have hardly sat down when I shout.

'If I ever catch the fella that's doing this, that's telling the lies, I'll bate the lard out of him and kick his arse out the door and he'll never again come near us.'

I'm saying it and I realize that this is the sort of thing that could set a room laughing. But not a flicker of a smile from any of the lads. Nobody would dream of leaving the side down.

Darragh Ó Sé and Seamus played especially well today. As we were coming up the stairs, I happened to be beside Darragh and gave his sleeve a tug.

'Darragh, you have a big part to play here. You were a leader on the field today, we need you to be a leader in this room now.'

I said the same thing to Moynihan. The boys played well. It gives them the moral authority to talk. Darragh stands up and speaks well. He backs what I say about doing violence to anyone who leaks lies to the papers. He talks about togetherness and sticking with each other. Coming from Darragh, that is great. He has burned the boats.

Seamus says something that nobody else would have the authority to say. He says that it was only a Munster championship. Everyone in the room has Munster medals. The year was always about winning the All-Ireland in September.

A sudden feeling comes over us: the pressure is off. The criticism we've been getting has done the work of ten sports psychologists.

Declan speaks, but his heart isn't in it. He's a broken wheel tonight. The lads can see he's hurting and it pulls them together tighter. We spent all of 2005 looking for this feeling of unity and purpose and we've found it in this room.

The owner of the Hayfield Manor, Joe Scally, tells Ger a story later in the summer about seeing us leave that room, seeing the looks on the players' faces, and calling a few friends and suggesting they put money on Kerry to win the All-Ireland. Sean Walsh is filled with the spirit, too. Sean tells anyone who will listen that we will win the All-Ireland.

We hang around the hotel for a meal and some drinks. I duck in and out with the players. I've talked with the selectors and things have become more clear. I find Donaghy and tell him that he will be going in at full-forward the next day. It's funny, but the suspension he served out today let Tommy Griffin in, and Tommy has done well. We know that midfield will cope without Donaghy.

I sit with Declan and tell him the bad news. He will have to be taken out of the firing line. He says there's two weeks to go before the Longford game, don't decide.

It's not a form thing, though. Whether he is going good or bad, he'll have to be taken out. We're fighting a losing battle. Being booed off the field by his own people after what he's given to Kerry is a shock and a scandal. To make matters worse, I know in my heart that they are booing Declan as a means of getting to me.

We get a couple of pints and wander out to the hotel garden and sit down under a tree. I've known Declan so long but we seldom get to talk much any more. He lives in Tralee and we pass at training and listen to each other make speeches in dressing rooms, and that's it.

We down the pints slowly, talking about the summer, about

football, about the old days in Coláiste na Sceilge. When we come back in, the lads are gone. The bus is gone. Everyone has baled off without us.

Ger (the haydog!) has ordered the bus to hit the road without even noticing the captain and manager aren't on it. The first he realizes is when I call him on the mobile when they're twenty miles down the way! It takes €100 worth of taxi ride for us to catch up with them all again, back in Killarney. Thanks, Ger.

In Killarney it's Tatler's Pub. On the night stretches, on and on. A great night. A thousand bonding exercises wouldn't bring a team together like the day we've had. Beaten by our neighbours, booed by our own and realizing in the end that we have the power to change it all ourselves.

Bits of the evening float around in my head. Darragh in fine form, grabbing my shoulder and leaning in to make some point over all the racket. Seamus tugging me by the wrist to get me away to make a more private, more earnest point in some corner. The usual giddy stuff you get when a team goes out drinking together.

I remember those little cameos mainly because the next week, through the kaleidoscope of the Sunday papers, it becomes gospel truth that Seamus had to pull myself and Darragh apart before we did damage to each other. They have it that things were so bad within the camp that Declan and I refused to travel with the rest of the team back to Killarney.

There is such a poisonous atmosphere around the place. The poison gets magnified and turned around on us in the papers. Stories that the Sé's have been attempting to pick the team. Walk-outs. Bust-ups. Attempted coups. You could go into every story and knock it on the head, but why dignify bullshit like that?

There's kicks in the *cojones* on every page I look at. I'm a man blinded by my loyalty to Declan O'Sullivan and I'm bringing this whole divided, disillusioned Kerry team to the grave with me.

There's a story of tensions between West and South Kerry players, a dumb allegation that Declan O'Sullivan will only pass to Paul O'Connor. This is supposedly on the basis that they are both from South Kerry. They're not. Paul is from Kenmare.

There's a story back home about why one of the cliffs over Coomasatharn Lake is known as Sagart. Back in Penal times, a priest was being chased by the English under threat of death for having said a Mass. He galloped his horse up the mountain and leaped off at the spot known as Sagart. Priest and horse dropped to the valley below. Sometimes I know how he feels. It would be easier to just take the leap.

One thing is for sure: somebody is feeding all this to the newspapers, somebody who gets calls from journalists. I don't know what their interest is in doing this but I'm fairly sure a lot of it is coming from Killarney and I'm sure it's done on the basis that they think I'm dead in the water as a manager.

Different things keep me going. Bloody-mindedness. Determination. This feeling of closeness with the team. And the perspective that comes in from the real world.

The day after the replay in Cork, on the Monday morning a friend of mine, Oliver Walsh, who used to play with me in Dromid, got killed on the way to work with his brother. They crashed on the road between Cahirciveen and Glenbeigh.

Oliver's mother has a way with words and she once composed a song about me after the 2004 All-Ireland final. When we brought the cup back to Dromid it was sung to the air of 'The Langer'! They had a local musician, Dominic O' Sullivan, up on the stage in Dromid singing it.

I'd been talking to Oliver on the previous Friday night at the regatta in Ballinskelligs. Oliver's car crashed into the back of a trailer of turf. Now there's a little monument on the side of the road to Oliver that I pass every night on the way to training.

Oliver's death is another poignant moment in this strange year. It's a reminder that life can be short and we just have to keep on. Oliver won't see another match.

I've told Declan that we will be taking him out of the firing line, but as the following week wears on and I brood more on the booing of the Kerry captain my feelings change a bit. I'm angry and defiant. I want to stick a finger up to them. No way will I let the bastards who did that beat us. I ring the chairman. I'm seething with rage and I tell him I don't give two damns about the faceless bullies up in the stand. I won't be dropping Declan. Sean, like a wise man, does the right thing and says very little. He just lets me get rid of the bit of steam.

He is right, too. When I calm down and think about it, I know I am fighting a losing battle. We have to let Declan find some form, and find himself. Right now, I can see he is lost psychologically, he's not sure what is happening. This is as rough as it gets for a young player, and Declan is young. I remember the night back in 2004 when Dromid won the South Kerry championship, ensuring that Declan would become captain of Kerry the following year. Declan had an All-Ireland medal from that September, he had a county medal with South Kerry and a South Kerry medal with Dromid, won that day. It was 18 December, and it was his twenty-first birthday.

Now we are in tatters. There is so much negativity going around that I have banned it. I don't want to hear it. I have my hands over my ears. Declan Coyle has warned me: people are either filling your bucket or they're emptying your bucket. The ones who are emptying it are the energy vampires.

I need to keep the positivity as high as possible. A couple of people who mean well ring me up and ask me about rumours they've heard. Gently I've had to ban them. This summer I don't do negativity!

My days have a pattern now. I've discovered a *poll gorm* down near Culloo on Valentia Island. The tide comes in over the rocks, and when it goes out it leaves a pool of completely natural salt water, nicely heated by the morning sun. I'll drive over and hit a few golf balls on the commonage in Paris and then jog down to the *poll gorm* and have a swim. Then jog back and stop off in the Skellig Mist coffee shop or The Bridge Bar in Portmagee for a cappuccino and a read of the papers.

I'll then head to training, as relaxed as can be, actually looking forward to the journey up to Killarney and the company of my thoughts.

Even back in the winter and through the dog months of the

league I'd be on long walks. I'd head from the house, branch off back left around a tight hairpin and shoot back to Glen Iarrach, away up over the sea, looking at the lights of the Glen and the moon picking out the shadows of the Skelligs. Nourishment for the brain. I get my kicks out of that. Exercise.

Most winter days when I'd knock off school, if there was no training I'd have a bit of lunch in Cahirciveen and then head out to Father's in Toorsaleen. I'd have a cup of tea with him, tog out and go way up the mountain for a couple of hours. I'd go in to the hills on big walks. Nobody within an ass's roar. I can leave a howl or a curse out into the forestry above me and nobody will hear me. The solitude is fantastic. Listen to the radio on the old Walkman, get lost in my thoughts. It insulated me and strengthened me.

Then I'd come back down, maybe bed for an hour, shoot the breeze with Father, maybe some supper, swipe a couple of organic eggs from the yard and away home. Might be seven or eight at night by the time I'd go home. I was neglecting my own gang a small bit, but I was doing everything right. At night I'd read to relax myself. Bits of autobiographies mainly, just looking for little nuggets I could steal.

A year of being halfway to full time at this job has shown me the difference between the amateur and the professional. It's almost a mental health issue.

The team is moving with one metabolism after the Cork defeat. Management is happy. The players are happy. They have a decent game with Longford to come. They have a new full-forward. The world has a different version of things, but screw the world.

We have a meeting one evening in the Brehon Hotel, and Moynihan speaks about the ferocious stuff going on about us all, the sheer strangeness of being in the middle of this whirlwind of rumours and negativity. He speaks about togetherness and not letting the side down and that being the only way to get through it.

We just keep going. When we got together for training on the

Tuesday after Cork, I asked Donaghy to go and stand beside Marc Ó Sé on the edge of the square while I landed a few balls in on top of them.

I was impressed. Walking to the dressing room, I asked Marc if he was impressed, too.

'He's deceptively fast,' says Marc, who is exceptionally fast himself.

'Hmmm.' Big and fast. We could be on to something a bit different here.

A night or two later, the full-forward thing isn't just an idea, it's the whole future. I ask Donaghy what sort of ball he thinks he'd like sent in.

'Just float in high, diagonal ball that I can attack,' he says.

I walked away, wearing a grin that ran from ear to ear. You hear a big, tall full-forward with character talk seriously about 'attacking' the ball and you know that you're in business. Height, pace, strength, agility, football ability. Hallelujah. The kid is an iceberg. The football world will get to see the tip of the iceberg over the next few weeks.

When we have our full-scale games of Gaelic football, Donaghy looks exciting at full-forward. He has made a huge difference to Gooch and Mike Frank, and they both look very good. Mike Frank came on as a sub in the replay in Cork and kicked a great score. Gooch, Donaghy and Mike Frank – this is our inside line now. I would not have believed that possible a few weeks ago.

Maybe this September will be the first All-Ireland week where I get to give good news to Mike Frank.

We've had a good time of it since the defeat. There's something about being put against the wall to face the firing squad that's liberating. We've brought in Botty O'Callaghan from Killarney (he's sort of a town councillor-cum-DJ, is Botty) because we felt we needed somebody around the place to organize stuff. Just bibs and water and extra ice for the ice baths. He is fantastic. Very positive. Good with the lads. He has fitted in with our new mantra about just enjoying whatever is left of the season.

He's very positive. And Donaghy, with a new job to do and a

bit of status within the team, is emerging as a huge asset, too. He just has this great open personality that lets you know he's enjoying everything and that it's only a game and why wouldn't you enjoy it.

Being thrown in at full-forward to save the season for a county that is hooked on negativity doesn't bother him a bit. We look at him some evenings and wonder why, if it doesn't bother Donaghy, it should ever bother us.

17

A Dub wouldn't be overly conscious of how many northsiders or southsiders Paul Caffrey might have on his panel. In Kerry, with the divisional system and the rivalries within that, everyone is conscious of how their men are doing. Football is politics here.

When I was working with Páidí in South Kerry I was viewed as the South Kerry selector. When I came back in as a selector in 2000, I was expected to root for our man. Our man was Maurice Fitzgerald. The problem was that, much as I admired Maurice Fitz, I'd got it back loud and clear from the remaining selectors when I came into the job for the second time that Maurice had been drifting for two years and that he was going to struggle to get back to his 1997 form.

I suspected as much. He hadn't set the world alight in 1998, and Brian Lacey marked him well against Kildare in the semi-final that year. The next year, Ronan McCarthy of Cork wrapped him up (literally at times) on a bad day when Kerry scored just 2–4 in the Munster final.

And his body language suggested he wasn't happy. Maurice comes over as a shy person, he doesn't speak to the media and keeps himself to himself, but he has a huge belief in his own ability. Like any elite athlete he knows what is best for himself.

He broke his leg in August, back in Gallarus. And then, come the new year, he tore into the training with a new resolution, but unfortunately he broke the leg again in Killarney in January. He'd done a long hard run on the Saturday with John O'Keeffe on Banna Beach and then broke the leg, playing a bit of football, the next day. He was fighting an uphill battle with the injury, so when the season came around it was complicated. We felt that he didn't have enough training to justify the starting position. And of course after that, the less he played the less chance he had.

Anyway, we liked him coming off the bench. He scored a goal in the drawn Armagh game when he came on. In the replay, his pass to Mike Frank, forty yards off the left foot, sticks in the mind of anyone who saw it. Eye-of-the-needle stuff.

So we came to the All-Ireland final. All over Kerry there was talk of nothing else but Maurice Fitz. With Maurice, the more tranglam and racket there is surrounding him, the harder it gets to tell what he's thinking. I remember in 1997 wondering about the pressure on him. Kerry had no All-Ireland in eleven years. The whole town of Cahirciveen was like a shrine to the prophet. He was the saviour. On the morning of the final we went down for a warm-up in Blackrock College. Maurice was sauntering around in his runners, kicking a few frees. He kicked a sideline with his left foot just wearing his runners, and then he did the same in the final that afternoon. No bother.

(That afternoon in Croke Park, under the greatest expectation and pressure imaginable, Maurice didn't touch the ball for the first fifteen minutes. His first contribution was to accidentally break Billy O'Shea's leg. He then proceeded to give an exhibition. Nine points to end the famine. Imagine the mental strength of the man.)

On the night the team was announced for the 2000 final, Maurice saw red. In South Kerry the pressure is on me now. Why is Maurice Fitz not in? You're letting us down!

A few days later, I gave Maurice a call to see if he was in. I told him I'd call down to the house. We were sitting in the kitchen talking it through, me explaining the selectors' thinking, Maurice nodding doubtfully, when his father Ned came in the door. Ned gave me blue murder. Locally, because of his hair and dark complexion, some comedian gave Ned a new name, Don King. I felt like one of Mike Tyson's victims by the time I got out of there. I gave a bit back but I didn't appreciate the verbal ambush.

By the time we got to Dublin, things were bad. Maurice and I had a rumpus up in the bar of the Hogan Stand after the drawn game against Galway in the final. He had been brought on as a sub all right, but in the wrong position.

There had been a row on the sideline. There was the usual fuss, with five selectors each trying to look after their own patch and John Crowley ended up being the fall guy. That meant Maurice Fitz going into the corner, a spot that he's never had the pace for. Madness.

We were all tense and frustrated. A drawn All-Ireland final leaves you drained but knowing you have to start up again. Then it all broke out upstairs in the Hogan half an hour later. Not the place or the time, but Maurice was furious and I was still livid over being ambushed by his father. I told him I didn't appreciate him just sitting there serenely while the selector he was supposedly depending on to fight his corner was being abused.

He came on then on the forty, where it suited him, in the replay and he did very well. It wasn't enough in Kerry, though. Maurice Fitzgerald wasn't in the photo of the starting fifteen on All-Ireland day.

On the morning of the 2000 final one of the papers ran an article by Mick O'Connell lacerating the Kerry management team over Maurice Fitz. Connell would have seen Fitzy as a reflection of himself, a supreme stylist who he had a hand in nurturing. When push comes to shove, it comes back to your own patch of grass, though. Not the green and gold. The fields around you.

Or maybe Mick just needed to make the point that the *cabóg* from Dromid was to blame!

The Kerry public felt a little cheated. They wanted to see Fitzie's class on show. All that the management was interested in was winning. The more rumpus there was about Maurice Fitzgerald, the more management felt backed into a corner. In fact his champions did him more harm than good. Looking back, it all seems like a sort of craziness. It just grips you, though. A season has its own logic and you just go with it most of the time.

The team for the Longford game is being picked tonight. We've looked at Longford v. Derry on video. They are very lively up front. Barden and Kavanagh move around a lot. We've done a lot of one-on-one stuff with the backs. Word is that the whole of Longford has gone mad. There'll be a good atmosphere in Killarney, I hope.

After we've picked the team I have a few pints with Jerry Mahony in the Royal Hotel in Valentia. He sees signs of hope. Donaghy at fourteen. Griffin in midfield. If it works out it will change the face of the season, he says.

Overall, things have gone well in the big build-up. There's been a good attitude from players, except for Tomás Ó Sé, who doesn't look tuned in.

I have a spat one evening with Tomás. A stupid thing. The whole mantra for the week is Donaghy. Either he works or we sink. We have tunnel vision. I'd said this in the Hayfield Manor. We have to get a primary ball-winner inside. I'd said it to the press, never mind to the players. Our whole play was gone static and sideways.

I was going to be pushing this Donaghy thing for the five sessions we had before playing Longford. Since we'd heard the draw, we were concentrating on quality of ball to Donaghy. Quality! I looked out a few times and Tomás was soloing upfield with the ball and not releasing it when he should have been. I got cranky. I dived straight in.

I had a bit of an altercation with him. I knew straight away that I had handled it badly that evening. I dived in with the studs up. I was under pressure, he was under pressure, and I'd made a balls of it.

Shit. I know that right now I am obsessed about getting the ball in to Donaghy but we'll sink or swim on our ability to do that. Part of Tomás's natural game though is driving out with the ball. He's being asked to sacrifice that, and I have been aggressive and cranky about it.

Better news is that the Gooch has been very lively this week. With Declan dropped, there's no South Kerry player on the team, so Gooch is captain. A turn of the captaincy will inspire him, maybe.

I've given Gooch the job of coaching Donaghy. Gooch wants

some muscle in there. In exchange he has to coach Donaghy on the run. The Gooch has forgotten more about forward play than most lads will ever remember. He just knows where to be, two or three passes ahead. Donaghy is manna from heaven for Gooch.

I still think Declan is our forty-yards man if he can get his confidence back. He won't play against Longford, though. We need to press Longford high up the pitch. They like playing around with the ball. I have to be very specific in instructions to every player. No point being woolly with them any more.

When the day comes, a perfect Saturday afternoon at the end of July, it all goes like clockwork. Kerry 4–11, Longford 1–11.

In the first fifteen minutes we score three goals. It gets the doubtful Kerry public on our side straight away. Bang! Bang! Bang! Donaghy works like a dream. He's involved in all four goals.

(Afterwards I spot him in the sunshine outside the dressing room, surrounded by journalists and chatting away happily. I've half a mind to haul him inside. A young player talking to journalists! What next! I leave him there, though. His positive nature is infectious. It can carry us for a while now till the energy vampires leave us alone.)

Donaghy prospers but our backs are in trouble. Seamus is opened up by Barden. Tomás isn't great and we take him off with about fifteen minutes to go. For all our good play, they were cutting through us a bit around that part of the field.

Tomás headed out to the dressing room like a madman. He was gone out the gate before we even got back in. We needed that like a hole in the head.

The story was that we were in disarray. We'd kept the lid on any real differences we'd had up to here. And now, right here in Killarney, we'd screwed it up. Even after a fine win there'll be more conspiracy theories doing the rounds tomorrow.

We had a meal back in the Towers Hotel and then went into a room across in the Plaza and had a meeting. Tomás wasn't there, of course. He'd gone home and was halfway to Cork at this stage. I've said so often that, however cranky a player is, we can have no shows of dissent. If you're angry, talk to me.

The whole theme now is that we have a week for Armagh. Can't drink! Eat properly! Hydrate properly! Rest properly! One week for Armagh!

I'm on the way home and I'm thinking to myself this is a bad, bad one. More garbage hanging over us. Losing one of the Sé's would be a disaster. The press will pick this one up. I'd better deal with it quickly.

I sent Tomás a text in the morning: 'Tomás, we need to talk.'
Text back.

'Fair enough. Meet you in the Park Hotel on Tuesday evening before training.'

I took off from Finan's Bay an hour and a half early. Into the hotel and sat down. Nice little spare room they have, soft seats. I often use it. I'm a bit *piseogach* about things myself. I stick to the same spots.

I said to him, 'Tomás, look, I'm here to listen to you, because what happened the last day isn't good for any of us.'

He proceeded to explain it all. It opened my eyes a bit more. It brought it home even more acutely how badly I had handled it all. I had been under pressure, I'd been cranky. He thought I brought the bit of aggro we'd had into the decision to bring him off. He thought there were one or two other fellas who maybe were worse than him against Longford.

Fair enough. I realized I'd handled it badly but I didn't bring any agenda into the game. I handled it badly in the previous training session.

When you have these meetings, the player has got to feel that he is getting something out of it. It takes a while to learn that. You give a little. We shook hands and said we'd get on with it. As we were walking out Tomás said to me that he wanted to play against Armagh as badly as anyone. He reminded me that he lost the 2002 final to them.

So we left feeling good. I asked Tomás to say something to the team at the end of training. If you storm off like that, it's a bit disrespectful to the guy who's coming on. There'd be a situation at the end of training where he could say a few words.

We had a very good training session that evening. The boys were in good form. We felt the season was turning. Up in the corner we had our usual chat as we were stretching.

Tomás said, 'Lads, I was a bit out of order the last day. I was mad and I took off into the dressing room and I was no sooner in the dressing room than I knew I was wrong. I fucked off out the gate and it's not far to the car once you're out the gate. Listen, lads, the good thing about Croke Park is I won't have the car there.'

He gets a round of applause. It turns a delicate situation into something great, shows the real human side to Tomás. The season is coming together. We can win this.

The Armagh game is six days away. Suddenly we're looking at the field for the rest of the All-Ireland championships and thinking that if we can get past Armagh, there's a chance of winning the thing. Tyrone have gone. On a day in early July, racked by injury, they got caught by Laois in a qualifier game. Of sides we want to settle up with, there are two left. Armagh and Cork. It suits us fine.

In Coláiste na Sceilge we accepted what had happened to us on that April Fools' Day in Limerick. We were young and we were optimistic. It was an adventure and a journey. The boys were so into this trip we were on together, that five or six of them decided to repeat their Leaving Certs the next year. We would have ten of the team back for another crack at the Hogan Cup.

More than that, of course, we were fanatical. And we watched out for each other.

For instance, Declan went off the rails a bit when he was about seventeen years old. He was getting a bit of a name around the place. He was drinking more at seventeen than he drinks now, but it's hard for young lads growing up in a place like this. Jack O'Shea did the same when he was that age, just went off the rails for a short while in Cahirciveen.

I took Declan away for lunch one day when he was in Leaving Cert. year and we sat down in the Ringside Rest and talked. We knew each other very well by then, so there was no beating around the bush. I told Declan that I'd come across plenty of lads with his sort of ability who had never made it because they didn't look after themselves. Something Alex Ferguson used to say to young lads at Old Trafford came into my head. Don't have fellas coming up to you in ten years' time telling you, 'You could have made it, you could have been something.' Declan had all the tools for greatness. He was a Kerry minor and a Kerry Under-21 by then, and in Dromid he was our hope for the future.

He got back on track.

Then there was Declan's buddy and comrade, Jer O'Shea. Young Jer had his own troubles. In the country, in the bleakness of South Kerry especially, the desolation can seep into your head.

Jer had lost his brother Tom a couple of years earlier and the pain of it was often there on Jer's face.

That second year, when we were once again going for the Corn Uí Mhuirí, Jer had been in hospital for a bit. He was a bright guy, a lovely presence in the team, and I remember at training in the run-up to Christmas he just wasn't the best. Then one day he was gone. The lads said Jer was in the hospital in Tralee. He wasn't just the type of player we would miss in games; he was the type of kid you'd miss at training.

I rang him in Tralee around Christmas and told him that we were having our last training session of the year during the Christmas holidays and a meal afterwards in the Sceilig Rock in Cahirciveen. Our bus driver, Eileen Clifford, had sponsored the night out. Without Jer there, it wouldn't be the same for anyone. He promised he'd come.

He made it out and I remember that night well. Jer was a little bit down in himself still. A small bit subdued and we were trying to support him. The lads were building him up and I was touched by it. That sort of support and love was there between them all, and it's a rare thing in young fellas.

We had Jer back with us and we had the passion about that Hogan Cup holding us together. I went out that same winter and bought €4,000 worth of weights with my own money. I got a lot of it paid for by sponsors afterwards (local businessman Tom Keane was very generous) but at the time I just said fuck it, we'll do whatever it takes to win this.

The boys, they trained like dogs that year. They were lads, all sixteen, seventeen or eighteen, and they gave up going out. There were so many Sunday morning sessions, never a thought among them of going out on Saturday night. What stood out in those seasons was the work we did over Christmas time. We used to train on St Stephen's Day, New Year's Day and in between on the 27th or 28th of December too. They were eating fruit, drinking orange juice, looking after themselves and working out, every chance they got.

We'd go up to the beach at Rossbeigh for three or four sessions at Christmas. Nine in the morning they'd be up with the gear on, ready to meet the bus and go to the dunes. Up those sand dunes. Down again. Fellas vomiting. Fellas collapsing. Along the beach, spread out like thirty-five lunatics just running in the wind. Some days it was survival of the fittest – keep going till the last man falls.

Going back to the club scene afterwards, it was primitive for them, they said. The old run-a-few-laps-and-play-a-game sessions. In their free time in school they'd go and pump weights. They fed off it and each other. The thought of winning the thing drove them. There were two roads they could have gone down after they lost to St Pat's. If you're young and you've never lost, you play without fear, you just go out and play with your instincts. Or being beaten can knock the life out of a team. They'd had the life knocked out of them and they'd stood back up again.

They were mad to prove a point.

We won the Munster Championship again. Our goalie, Bryan Sheehan, came down the field and scored a goal with a last-second free kick in the semi-final against a Killorglin team that had six or seven Kerry minors on it. Jer O'Shea was back with us and he scored our other goal that day. I remember saying to the lads before the game that if we beat this Killorglin team it would take a great team to stop us.

In the Corn Uí Mhuirí final we beat Coláiste Chríost Rí of Cork. Munster champions again. The semi-final with St Jarlath's of Tuam was fixed for April in Limerick. St Jarlath's had just won the their fourth Connacht title on the trot and at the time had eleven All-Ireland wins already under their belt.

There were 7,000 people at the semi-final with Jarlath's, although many more now claim to have been there. When people talk about the greatest game of colleges football ever played, that afternoon always gets a mention. Ninety minutes of football, including the extra time. Forty scores. All points. Thirty-seven of them from play. Twenty of them for Jarlath's and twenty of them for us. Only once all day was there more than a point between the two of us. The sides were level seventeen times. The football was brilliant. For all of us involved and for all who genuinely saw it, this WAS the greatest game ever played.

A week later, we were in Limerick yet again for the replay. We were on a double bill with a hurling game, and there were 20,000 people there this time.

Five points up halfway through the second half, we lost a little confidence and found ourselves a point down coming into the final minutes. Then lightning struck in the same place as it had a year previously. Joe Corridan got a goal for us and we were two points ahead as the game went into injury time.

Then a high ball came into our square from their wing-back and the Jarlath's midfielder, Damien Dunleavy, went up and punched it to the net. It was the clearest square ball I have ever seen, but referee Brian White gave the goal. This happened in the same goalmouth on the same pitch as the St Pat's incident a year before.

We came back and Adrian Breen our midfielder scored an extraordinary point from sixty yards to draw the game. The final whistle blew and there was chaos.

I was carried away with rage. I stormed on to the pitch to have a go at Brian White. I don't even know if it was Brian or the umpire who made the call on the Dunleavy goal. I just know that it was allowed. Declan was there beside me as we argued.

What's the point. We'd been screwed again. The game was going to extra time.

There was a debate over extra time. The St Jarlath's coach, Father Oliver Hughes, came over to us and, in a sporting gesture that is the mark of the man, said that if we didn't want to play extra time, St Jarlath's wouldn't push the case. We'd come back another day and play each other.

I looked at the boys as Father Oliver walked away. I wanted extra time. I told the team that there'd be no justice in the world if we lost.

'Lads, if there's a God there, it'll work out for us. We've been screwed again, but, boys, we'll go out and we'll play it. Point for point. Score for score. This will work out.'

We lost it by a point. I felt as if I'd been hit with a massive sledgehammer. I remember seeing Father Oliver Hughes in the middle of the field. I went to embrace him and he was crying like a baby. And he'd won.

I had to turn and face our dressing room. I'd told the boys in there to play extra time, I'd told them to trust me. It didn't work out. I had played my last card with them and let them down. I stood outside the dressing room for a minute and wondered how I would explain myself. It didn't work out after all, did it, boys?

I walked into the most devastated dressing room I have ever been in. Two years of our lives, and the boys hadn't an ounce left to give. It's a cliché sometimes, but this is more than a game. It was a while before I could speak.

I told them that this is life. Sometimes things don't work out. The tears rolled down my face, looking at them. No more to say. We'd move on. Declan stood up and he spoke about friendships. This is a young fella in a dressing room on the worst day of his life, and it was beautiful.

There we were, a roomful of broken boys. And myself and my two trusty lieutenants, John Noel O'Shea and John Dorgan. Everyone crying and emotional. I was trying to make sense of it when Barney O'Reilly, the chief executive of the Vocational Schools in Kerry, came in the door. Barney is an academic man and I thought that whatever he'd say would be inappropriate. I was wrong. Barney made a hugely emotional speech in the middle of the floor about how proud he was of us. He told the boys what they had come to mean to the people of Kerry. Lovely words.

And then Jer O'Shea stood up.

Jesus, it stays with me forever. Jer, this cheerful young fella who was the life and soul of the team but who had so much going on in his young head. It would never occur to you sometimes that he would have any troubles, that there was anything but football in his life. He stood up and he talked about the team. He talked about the meal we'd all had together at Christmas. He talked about what being involved had given him. He said thank you. When he was finished there wasn't one of us not looking at the floor with the tears dropping down between our feet.

I tried to rationalize it all afterwards. I went home and looked at the video. The square-ball decision wasn't even debatable. I got a copy of the video and I rang Brian White's number.

I said, 'Brian, I'm not giving out to you but I have to get it off my chest. We've given two years to this and one of your umpires has cost us a Hogan Cup. I'll send you the video. Have a look.'

So I posted off the video to Brian White. I did no more, but I needed to do that. No hard feelings. In the years afterwards I have developed a great relationship with Brian.

Back then it just hurt, though. These kids had been together so long. They'd been the South Kerry representative team from the age of fourteen, when they'd won the county title and Jer O'Shea had been top scorer. They'd won three minor titles together and three Under-21s as well, outside the school.

Yet, of the boys, only Declan and Bryan Sheehan ever went on to wear the green and gold at senior level. A few played minor and Under-21, but that was it.

Kieran Cronin got a bad injury playing with the Kerry Under-21s. A belt in the back which left him for the bones of six weeks in the rehabilitation centre in Dun Laoghaire in Dublin. He lost partial use of his left hand and could never play again. He's in Australia now.

A lot of the other guys don't play much any more. Compared to that Jarlath's team, it is disappointing. Fellas like Gary Sice, Niall Coleman, John Devane and Michael Meehan have all gone on to be seniors for Galway. Several more have played Under-21 football in the maroon.

Some of the lads still play socially. One or two, like Wayne O'Sullivan who marked Michael Meehan in those games, would be on South Kerry sides; but mostly they were lads who played their part, who played above themselves on a team which was special.

The two great stars of the colleges game at that time were Michael Meehan and Declan. They both played full-forward then, and the semi-final was seen by some as a showdown. Michael Meehan won out, I suppose, but Declan has two senior All-Irelands since then. I know that occasionally he still measures his progress against Michael's.

Declan broke through on to the Kerry senior team in 2003. They won a Munster title that year. They played Roscommon in the All-Ireland quarter-final. Late in the week before the game, I was up the back of the house, putting out washing, hanging up sheets and towels, when Declan called me.

He was very upset, hardly able to get the words out. Jer O'Shea had taken his own life. He was gone at twenty years of age, gone the same way and at the same age as his brother, Tom.

Declan and Jer would have been very close. They came up together, shared so many dressing rooms and played so many hundreds of games beside each other that they knew each other inside out. In the end they played minor for Kerry together in a team that included the Gooch.

Declan scored a goal for Kerry against Roscommon in Croke Park that weekend. First thing he did was to look up to the sky and say, 'Jer boy, that's for you.'

Every day since, every big game when he's listening to '*Amhrain na bFhiann*' or walking the parade, he looks up and talks to his old friend. 'Jer, look out for me today, man.'

Jer would never tell anyone when he was going through a rough patch, but Declan would know. They had an intuition with each other on and off the pitch. The death of Jer's brother, Tom, was the first big tragedy to touch most of the boys. That shook them up as sixteen-year-olds, brought them all closer. Declan and Jer went through it together as friends.

You'd hear stories of Jer's troubles. Once, in a bar, Declan got a call to tell him that Jer had died. Declan doubted it and the first thing he did was call Jer's phone. Jer answered.

'Is everything okay?'

'Yeah, Dec.'

'Jesus Christ, man.'

That's how it was with Jer.

You start blaming yourself for small things. A week or two before he was gone, I passed Jer on the road going down to

Waterville. The sun was in my eyes, he was waving to me and I was half past him before I knew who it was. It bothered me for a long time, that he might have thought that I'd have ignored him. That was the last time I saw him. On the side of the road, a dark figure set against the sun.

I never went into the hospital to see him. It's a delicate thing in a small community; sometimes things like that can be close to the bone for a family. You never know whether a family want everyone running in there or not. So I stayed away. Jer was very quiet when he came out at Christmas for that meal with us. I think, for Jer and the character he was, he was a little embarrassed. Yet the boys were so close as a team that I know he was comfortable and happy to be there.

It stays with me forever, that time and those moments. Jer standing up in that dressing room in Limerick and saying things that were more important than winning or losing. I knew then that it was about people as much as it was about anything else.

Jer wore his heart on his sleeve, but you could see the hurt in his face a lot of the time. His sister Martina tells me that in the last two years it was football that kept him going. His last game just before he died was maybe his greatest. He scored 1–6 for St Michael's, Foilmore, in the South Kerry league final in Cahirciveen. I heard that and smiled. Sweet left foot.

The next thing we knew was that he was gone and there was a space left in all our lives.

19

When we come back to Fitzgerald Stadium to train, four days after the Longford game, we are a different team. The weight is gone. We train quickly. Short, sharp and lighthearted.

Ger, my man with his ear to the players, has told me that by now they are a bit bored by the long meetings and the video analysis, so we keep it simple. We have sharpened everything, even me. I've just lightened up a bit and stopped overthinking it all. It's football! Let instinct take over.

Somewhere in all the poison and the despair we forgot that it's a long year. You can't keep the pedal to the metal the whole time. We went through a period when there was no spark. Nothing there. While we got ourselves interested part of the way for Cork, we couldn't get to the level.

It didn't register with me at the time, even though the other selectors were saying it to me, that these players were having a hard time getting motivated. A Munster championship wasn't going to do it for them. They had their eyes on the big canister.

So tonight we train quickly under the high windows of St Finian's and instead of going to a room for a meeting, I move some figures around a Subbuteo board for five minutes. It's a change. Everyone is on good form. Armagh focuses the minds without me having to make any effort.

We speak about Armagh for a few minutes, especially about Kieran McGeeney. Armagh have created a sense of myth around themselves. McGeeney is the best example. He is indestructible! He trains twice a day every day and then goes to the shops and spends thirty euros a day on fruit! And Francie Bellew is Cú Chullain. I give them a few instance of this, trying to demystify Armagh and the whole northern legend.

Brossy destroyed Kieran McGeeney in the first half in 2002, and

McGeeney has got no faster since. Stephen O'Neill destroyed Bellew last year in the Ulster final, I think it was. Bellew had to be moved off him. Our men can't do the same? Is anyone telling me that?

A big part of Armagh's success is this aura. They've turned around the GAA thing of playing yourself down. It's a brilliant move, but we have something to counter it.

There's an old story from home. Two men came to our valley, all the way from Glenbeigh, across the mountain. They came down Coomaspeara. It was night-time and it was raining heavily. At the time the locals had nothing, but the rancher families used the land all round to graze their own herds on. There were all kinds of animals there, and maybe it wasn't the first trip the two men had made because they knew where to look and what to do.

They found a fine cow and they killed it there in the moonlight. There were little stone huts for shelter on the side of the mountain and between them they manoeuvred the cow into one hut, hit her with a rock and began to cut her up. They skinned her, bled her and cut her up there on the mountain. Two starving men. They put the meat into a couple of large baskets that they hung from their necks and tried to get back to Glenbeigh before light. The rain was torrential and they lost sight of each other as they made their way down the mountain. Only one man made it back. The other got drowned, crossing the river at Caolgarbh. The waters were flood swollen. The rope twisted around the poor man's neck and he went under. Downriver, a day later, they saw blood in the water and a chunk of meat and the body of a man who died for his hunger.

Suddenly we have a hunger like that, a grim, raw hunger. We've been through enough for now. We've come out the other side and we know what we want.

I get help with statistics from John O'Dowd, an ex-*Kerryman* journalist who watches tapes of our games in Australia, where he now lives, and from Sylvester Hennessy, who does the game-day stats for *The Kerryman* and the same, with a few extras, for me. In the

Longford game Sylvester has been looking at Seamus Moynihan. Seamus had twenty-five possessions and he hand-passed twenty of those.

He has to kick the ball more. He has become overly conservative. That's the mark of his brain. He had a telepathic understanding with John Crowley and that ratio would have been the reverse when Crowley was there. Now, with no big man, he's gotten used to playing the percentages. We need him using his kicking for Donaghy, to open them up.

Seamus didn't play great against Longford, but the fact that he's playing at all is a wonder and a blessing for us. I remember some of the matches in 2005, the man could hardly tie his laces, he was in so much pain. Against Mayo he had to get physio just to go out again for the second half, but over the winter he went out and did the whole core-stability programme with Ger Hartmann. He did about forty gruelling minutes of tough work on his own every evening. He hasn't had a niggle all year. Pre-habilitation they call it.

I know the players notice that Seamus is practically undroppable. Tomás hinted as much when we spoke after the Longford game. Paul Barden took Seamus for three points from play that day. There's no forward who wouldn't be happy with that. There's no back who wouldn't notice it either.

Eamon Fitz could feel a bit hard done by. He won an All-Ireland in 2004 at centre-back, played there all the year, started there in 2005. And then in Seamus came, and Eamon lost out. He'd have felt that was tough, and it was. This year we started him at centre-back and he got a rough time from Ger Brady the first day out, so we stuck him up the other end as centre-forward.

Eamon has a lot of leadership qualities and he should establish himself again when Seamus goes. For the time being, it's difficult for him, though. Last year after the All-Ireland final I remember Eamon and I having a discussion.

'Jesus, Jack, the whole half-back line was beaten and I got five minutes as a sub?' Moynihan had been injured in the first round and Fitzie had got in and then lost out again. He felt a bit aggrieved.

'Listen, Eamon, at the start of this when I needed backing Seamus was there for me.'

'But Jack, sure we all backed you.'

'I know. I know. There's backing and there's backing, though. When the key man backs you, it's different. Seamus is Seamus.'

Eamon nods. That's why Seamus Moynihan will be Kerry manager some day soon: the authority he has in the county, the aura he carries with him, the example he gives.

I was a selector back in 2000 when we put him back in at full back. Having him in there was like having the world's finest tenor sing country music ditties, but that's what we needed. In the league quarter-final against Meath we conceded three goals and our regular number three, Barry O'Shea, had done his cruciate. Mike Mac wasn't the finished article then. Seamus went in and rescued us and, being Seamus, he won an All-Star in the position and Player of the Year.

We should have released him out the field after that, but we were conservative and, although we were missing what Seamus could do further up the field, no full back ever looked as good to us.

Moynihan can be a stubborn hoor. That's why he'll be a great manager. He can be stubborn but he'll learn his lessons quick enough. In the week before the Longford game, without giving him orders, we gently suggested that he not go down the field after Paul Barden when he roamed deep. We wanted Seamus to stay back and sweep. He wanted to go, though. He wanted to match him.

We were moving away from video analysis and just talking for five or ten minutes before or after a session. Barden is going to wander. We want Seamus to sit back; he wants to go and deny the bastard the ball. There's no point in me trying to get Seamus Moynihan to do something he doesn't want to do, but he's got bitten a bit in the game. Stung for three points. After that he could see where we were coming from.

He says it himself with a grin. Yeah, maybe it is better if I sit back and do some sweeping. That's what we want against Armagh.

There have been three landmark disasters in recent Kerry football history. Meath in 2001, where famously we selectors and Páidí just sat on the bench shaking our heads and hoping the earth would swallow us. Then Armagh in 2002 and Tyrone in 2003. And I suppose I have to add Tyrone in 2005.

Each one cut us deeply in its own way, but 2002 against Armagh went to the core of the team. In 2002, Kerry lost the Munster semi-final replay in Páirc Uí Chaoimh, just a couple of days after Darragh, Marc and Tomás had buried their father. The team went off out the back-door route and in the quarter-final against Galway they really threw off the shackles and played wonderful football, winning by eight points over the All-Ireland champions. Then Cork in the semi-final. Mike Frank scored 1–6. Gooch scored 1–5. There was fifteen points in it at the end.

Darragh was captain, and going into the final he was going to be Footballer of the Year. At half-time, with Kerry four points up, it was the same story. But Kieran McGeeney finished up with the Sam and the Player of the Year award. It's a game of inches, boys. In the second half that day Armagh said, what the hell, we'll throw the handle after the hatchet. They won by a point.

I was in the stand that day and you see things easier up there. If I'd had a line into the dugout that day, it would have been humming with the mantra, 'Kick the damn ball.' Now that we have the route into Donaghy I'm remembering those words.

Since then, despite our win in 2004, there is a perception that football has belonged to Armagh and Tyrone. They play their Ulster finals in Croke Park. They talk about football as if it was their own invention. In Kerry we are sidelined. We hate that. We're burning up with hunger this week. Things to settle when Saturday comes.

Diary entry:

Saturday 5th August: Game with Armagh on line with ten minutes to go. We're two points up. A man down. We score the next six. 1–3 without reply. What a day. One of the greatest days of my life. We wiped them out in the second half. Darragh Sé was majestic.

The sweetest day.

Armagh had us on the run in the first half. Standing on the sideline, it struck me early on that the football Armagh were playing was like something out of a coaching manual. McGeeney going back, cutting out the ball to Donaghy and coming out, delivering good ball. O'Rourke doing damage in the half forwards. Some of the best football I've ever seen.

The long diagonal ball works so well for them. I wandered the perimeter of the pitch, went behind the goal and looked upfield at one stage. Scary. Clarke and McDonnell were just flicking it. They have such telepathy. I came back to the bench and said to the lads that we had to tighten everything up back there. There's six or seven years of playing relationship going on in there with McDonnell and Clarke and it's frightening.

On the sideline I consulted with the selectors. That's one tough spot in there. We have to do something. We moved Marc out off McDonnell. Put Tom O'Sullivan back. Tom is such a laid-back bastard that nothing will faze him and we wanted Marc more in the game.

We tried to get Moynihan back to give cover. He dropped off McEntee, and what happened? McEntee lamped a point. Tommy Griffin was supposed to come back on McEntee. When McEntee scored his point, Moynihan cut his losses and went back out. So we had to let a half forward come back to midfield in order to allow Tommy Griffin to drop on to McEntee. In the second half we got it right. It worked.

We spoke at half-time about getting Moynihan back. Other fellas were to get a hand on McEntee. It's a case of tinkering with it all the time, tweaking it as we go. Only as the year has gone on have we got the system going where we can play Moynihan to his strengths. Once Seamus committed to the sweeping job, naturally he became brilliant at it. Joe Brolly picked it up in the analysis on the telly.

Marc had a brilliant second half in which he kicked two of the best points any back has ever kicked in Croke Park. Between those two points Tomás kicked one as well. Extraordinary men.

Darragh got a huge foothold in the middle. Galvin was tackling like a lunatic. He'd just turned them over for a point when another one of his turnovers led to Donaghy's goal, the score that swung the whole match.

Donaghy had been doing well on the legendary Bellew but not thriving. They were letting McGeeney come back to double-team him, but McGeeney was tiring. Donaghy wasn't getting any decisions and he was bellyaching a bit to the umpire. Paul Hearty, the Armagh goalie, was giving Donaghy a hard time, too. A big lank from basketball suddenly all over the papers? What else would you expect.

Late in the first half Gooch had a goal chance saved by Hearty. It led to a point by Franny. It took a bit of the sting out of Armagh. We got level, and then Donaghy's goal . . .

When Galvin turned it over, the ball came across to Seán O'Sullivan, who hit the perfect diagonal ball in to Donaghy. The trick with Donaghy has been getting the ball to him in basketball situations. On the hardwood he receives the ball with his back to the hoop and makes his move, driving in hard. He does just that now.

There's a memory, the story of the whole season. Francie Bellew on the ground behind Donaghy, the ball flying to the Armagh net past poor Hearty. Donaghy in Hearty's face with the immortal words, 'Who's crying now, baby!'

Donaghy's goal was a statement. Sticking the head into the *cúl báire*'s face.

Most of the time I'd try to keep myself calm on the sideline, but I let an old yahoo when I saw Donaghy. It felt like being set free.

There is a nugget in Brian Clough's autobiography that I applied to Donaghy. When Clough was starting his career as a player, he was in the reserves at Middlesbrough and waiting for his chance. He was getting cranky and impatient and finally the manager gave him his break and said to him just beforehand, 'I've given you a break, don't let me down.'

Worst thing he could say. You don't give players ultimatums or make it all about yourself. When we put Donaghy in at full-forward, we said to him that he was playing well in midfield, and that if this move didn't work, we'd put him out midfield again. No matter how he went, he wasn't going to make us any worse, and if he won just one ball out of every three that went in there, that would do us nicely. He discussed it with me afterwards and said it took the pressure off him.

After Donaghy put the ball in the Armagh net, fellas stuck out their chests. Everyone was playing now.

There's still part of me that's *piseogach*, though. Even when we're going well I'm waiting. I grew up in a place of curses. In my father's youth they used to run Biddy Balls in the local houses, where there'd be porter and dancing on the eve of St Brigid's Day. Then the local priest told them if it didn't stop he'd turn them all into hares. So it stopped. It makes a pessimist out of you, listening to those stories.★

Towards the end, when Paul Galvin lost his head and got sent off, I could see it slipping away from us. At the time the linesman on our side of the field seemed able to point the flag in only one direction. We were getting a bit wired up. There was an incident where John Toal, Armagh's *maor uisce*, appeared to provoke Galvin. The red mist descended and Galvin got stuck in by way of reply.

We were three points up. Three points up, with twelve minutes to go. Armagh came back and kicked another point quickly. Ten minutes to go and Armagh are a man up and it's their kind of scenario. We'll know now if all that we've been through has made a team of us again. This is what a season comes down to for any serious team. A time when the big question is asked.

The answer explodes out of us. All the shit and frustration is blown out in those last ten minutes. It's all working now. Fellas

★Some curses actually came true. The curses put on the landlords' agents who evicted tenants from land were especially common. The Lyons of Corabhuaile were said to be cursed. A widow with seven children was evicted out of there, and she knelt down at the gateway and cursed them that they'd be blind, lame and mad. Of the last generation, Mary was mad, Breege was blind and Fionan was crippled. Now the clan is gone.

coming back, covering, busting their guts. I look at Eoin Brosnan shadowing Paddy McKeever out to the end line, and when they get to the border of the pitch he fucks McKeever out over the end line. Men back working hard and fellas up front winning the ball. Aidan O'Mahony thundering into things. It's all unfolding in front of the eyes. Declan is on as a sub in the full-forward line and we can all see he's back on track. Bryan Sheehan kicks a great free to put us three up. Then, near the end, Darren O'Sullivan takes off. We knew that someday he was going to do this with his pace, and the day is now. He just burns through and scores a brilliant goal.

Altogether we score 1–3 without reply and end up winning the game by eight points. That maybe flatters us, but who cares. When it's over I should go to Joe Kernan and shake his gentleman's hand, but in the emotion of it all I take off for Darragh Ó Sé. All the *raméis* about us having an 'altercation' in Tatlers has made me feel close to him, and he was brilliant today, outplaying the other great midfielder of the decade, Paul McGrane. First thing he says to me is, 'Get the boys ready for Cork.' Funny thing is, Cork are only just coming out on to the pitch to play Donegal. But Darragh knows it's going to be Cork.

20

Back home again. We have a great and giddy week of training after Armagh. When you are winning games, your studs leave no marks in the ground. You just glide over everything. I watch the video of the game at least ten times, and it gets better each time. Our first taste of Croke Park this year and we put a lot of ghosts behind us.

There was a lot of emotion on the pitch and in the dressing room afterwards. I did an interview with Marty Morrissey. He was asking about trouble in camp. I was going to go into the angry old spiel, denying it all, but I just asked Marty what was wrong with fellas drawing a few clips on each other. Sure, that's what we're looking for!

We have Cork in our sights now – they did beat Donegal – and that's exactly the sort of game that we are looking for. If Donegal had beaten Cork I can't imagine the anticlimax it would have been for us. We want to give them a dose of our new system, let them get the backlash from our new sense of purpose. Nothing that happened in the previous two games will matter if we give them a decent beating in Croke Park.

You can see the confidence that winning brings to a team, especially to forwards. Gooch is a new man. Mike Frank is flying. On the Friday after Armagh we have a game in Fitzgerald Stadium among ourselves. The forwards move better than at any time in three years. They are awesome. They've suddenly realized it's all there for them.

I spoke to Ger Loughnane during the week. We met a year or so ago at a coaching conference in Tullamore. It was Ger who first introduced me to the idea of controlled aggression. He's an interesting man and I like to keep in contact and touch base with him. He'd had an article in the paper, talking about the hurling semi-final and how Clare would get hyped up to prove their critics wrong. Bad energy, he said. There's a bit of something in what Loughnane says.

Of course it's vital to concentrate on your own game, to play with steely focus and ruthlessness. That's what we're trying to do now. But shoving it to a few people along the way will be nice.

We have plenty of enemies still. We'll be well motivated for a while, using our good energy and our bad energy. Paul Galvin, for instance, has another name to add to his black book. He has been vilified. Joe Brolly had a cut at him on the television after the Armagh game, called him a corner boy and mentioned that he was a teacher. Brolly enjoys a good line, but this crossed a different sort of line.

Paul Byrne, the producer of *The Sunday Game*, was in touch with me. I think he was afraid we would withdraw our co-operation from RTÉ television. We could easily have done. That was the feeling. Brolly was out of order. Galvin is playing a game; bringing his profession into any criticism was wrong.

At this stage my old sparring partner Pat Spillane rang me. We talked, and Spillane gave Paul Galvin a bit of a break on the telly. We let it rest.

Meanwhile Darragh wants to make a statement against Cork's Nicholas Murphy. So far this season Murphy has caused us as much trouble as any other single player. Darragh didn't actually spend too many minutes playing directly on Murphy in either of the games because Murphy was playing on the forty, coming out to midfield when needed, and that was bothering us because the match-ups weren't right. After those first two games against Cork, there was an inaccurate perception out there that Murphy had outplayed Darragh twice. Every bone in Darragh's body wants Murphy now.

And personally I want to put one over on that other old buddy of mine, Billy Morgan, who's been bellyaching since the depths of winter about the sort of team we are. I think in his heart Billy will know now that the game is up. We've turned a corner. A third game is one too far for Cork. I hope so.

Things aren't good between us. I respect Morgan, but I think he sees me as a young manager that he can turn the heat up on. I didn't go into their dressing room in Páirc Uí Chaoimh after they beat us in the replay. I didn't see Billy in our dressing room either (but then again, I didn't see the Ó Sé's vanish out the door). I shook his hand at the end of the game. There's a famous picture. He's grinning. I look like I'm shaking hands but not feeling too good about the idea.

Play it as it lies! It's as if the whole thing has been scripted. Cork pulled their blatant stroke when they should have taken their beating on the Anthony Lynch issue in the drawn game. I remember looking at the mark on Donaghy's face when he came to training the following Tuesday and asking him if he was sure it wasn't the girlfriend, Hilary, that had hit him a poke the previous night. It must have been because, through some miracle of camerawork, Cork managed to 'prove' that it was only an attempted strike on Donaghy.

We felt very aggrieved. Anthony Lynch off playing in the replay, with Donaghy sitting in the stands. Now when we get Cork back to Croke Park we will be running out saying that by Jesus, Billy, if you're going to brand us for being cynical we might as well be hung for sheep as for lambs.

Karma. Donaghy getting sent off in the drawn match in Cork was a blessing for us. We got Tommy Griffin going. Donaghy might never have escaped from midfield but for that. Cork have had no luck since. Canty twisted his knee and is gone for the season. He's a huge loss to them.

For Sunday we've discussed our approach as a team. Morgan is still putting that fierce heat on referees, talking about us being cynical, etc. Refs will be reading this and saying, 'These guys are absolute lunatics.' We've decided in the end that, instead of going into our shell, as Morgan is hoping, we'll play right to the line. Our style will be: go to the point of fighting without actually fighting. There's a big difference.

Controlled fury is what we will hit Cork with. Some of our players can't play effectively any other way. That's Paul Galvin at his best. Darragh Ó Sé is the same. Right to the wire. Right to the borderline. In the Cork game they'll set the tone. Beating Cork in Croke Park in another big game (thirteen points in 2005, fifteen points in 2002) will send them home with a huge amount of self-doubt in their heads. That would be a decent season's work in itself.

Our objective is to get the lads playing with the relentless aggression we had after Donaghy's goal. John Corcoran has a piece in *The Kerryman* about what Cork will do to us. Thank you, John! *Is binn béal ina thost!*

The enthusiasm is everywhere. One evening, Franny and Gooch, Seán O'Sullivan and Donaghy come in to train on their own. Two of them kicking frees at one end of the stadium; Sean kicking long balls to Donaghy at the other end.

And Declan is working hard, too. After what happened in Páirc Uí Chaoimh he stepped back and decided he was going to work this out. I asked him, did he want sessions with Declan Coyle, but he has decided that there is only one way to move forward. He is going to prove it to himself and to the team. It would have cracked another young fella, what he went through, but Declan is meeting it head-on.

He's actually given up his job. He was working for Powerade on the road, and the job was taking him to Tipp and Limerick and other far-flung places during the day. He felt that it was taking a lot out of him that he could be putting into his football. He packed it all in, shortly after the second Cork game, and just vowed he'd do whatever it took. He's been phenomenal to watch. He's applied himself inside in training. We can see he has found his form. Meanwhile the lad is just living on what money he had saved. He has gone at football with a vengeance, looking to prove himself all over again to everybody. I've asked him a couple of times, did he need anything, but he has been determined to work it out on his own.

Darragh in particular has been very supportive to Declan. He'd say quietly to him after matches or training to keep working away, that it was going all right. I know this meant a lot to Declan. The opinions of the other players are what matter most in a situation like this, and Darragh is a huge figure to have encouraging you.

I don't know if earlier in the season there were any words between players about Declan's form. Declan would see himself as a forty-yard man, and the players would have known that. He was playing too deep when he was full-forward, not offering a target. I wasn't blind to that. I could see the ball wasn't sticking in there, and it was frustrating. To compensate, Declan was doing what a player who grows up as a star in a small club will sometimes do. He was overcarrying the ball, taking too much out of it.

Declan got a harder kick than most players will ever receive in their lives. I know the booing was meant for me when he was taken off in Páirc Uí Chaoimh, but that didn't make it any easier for a young man captaining his county. He came back though, he gave up his work, he trained hard, he never looked for favours from me or from anywhere else. He never bellyached to newspapers or chat rooms. There were no rumours about him. He played his football on the B team in training games and he regained the faith of his teammates. When you've been through the toxic summer that these fellas have been through, all that matters is the group who are inside the dressing room when the door is shut.

The people who booed in Páirc Uí Chaoimh only get to see what happens on the pitch. If it doesn't go as we had all hoped, it's my fault. If they could see what they did to a young player and if they could see the dignity and courage he has brought into fighting back, they'd be ashamed of themselves now.

Declan won't start against Cork, but he'll come on and play a part and have his chance to audition for the final. He deserves that. For character and for his play. And for all that we've been through together. Jer O'Shea can expect a call from his old friends.

For the game with Cork we have a new mantra. We're setting targets. Especially for the defence. We have to concede no more than five points a half. If the defence comes anywhere near those targets, I'm confident that the forwards will be cutting up down the far end.

Declan Coyle told me once that I should always speak to the soul of the team. He said that most of what managers say to players doesn't register with them. Only the passion and the demeanour seep through to the soul. In my first year, Kerry's soul was shrivelled from three years of beatings and criticism. We found a way through that because my voice was a novelty.

Last year we were on different pages. It was like trying to speak to somebody in a coma. They wanted to get better. I wanted them better. But there was no way of knowing if my words were even getting into their heads. As a team we tried to force things. We wanted it badly but not badly enough to burn the boats, not as badly as Tyrone did.

Now, though, we have been in the heat all summer. We've taken the worst in terms of the pressure cooker. We haven't cracked. At last again, when I speak to the team, I feel that every ear in the room is absorbing a little bit of what I say. There's stuff getting through to the soul. We enjoy being together. I feel that we've grown.

Take Darragh. Darragh has been happy this year. I don't know if it's the fact that he's getting married or that he has a new business, but he's happy in himself. I happened to be lucky in the Hayfield Manor that I was walking behind him on the way in and could ask him to carry the meeting. He'd played well. He was the king. He's a competitive hoor and the team love him and respect him for it.

By now I've learned that no team and no manager marches through the season to Croke Park. You tap-dance all the way. Not treading on this. Not splashing that. I read a book this year called *End the Struggle and Dance with Life*. In three years I've learned to dance like Astaire.

Kerry 0–16, Cork 0–10.

There was a moment early in the second half when Cork were three points down. They still had a chance to catch us and draw us into a dogfight. They looked odds-on to score a goal. Conor McCarthy had the ball on the edge of the square and he looked up for the hand-pass to Kevin McMahon, who was wide open and screaming for the ball. I was wondering where the cover was. We'd worked so hard on this over two weeks, and a goal for Cork at this stage would mean that our targets would be shot. Psychologically I didn't know what damage that would do.

The ball never got to McMahon's fingers, though. Seamus Moynihan exploded out of nowhere, clutching the ball to his gut, looking no different than he did when he was twenty-two or twenty-three. And a great roar went up from the green and gold in the stands. Maybe we're convincing them at last.

Getting through to a third All-Ireland final in three years would be enough convincing for any other county. I'd say Billy Morgan has gone home convinced. Billy was banished to the stand today for disciplinary reasons, and at one stage when a picture of his face came up on the big screen he looked so worried that there was a cheer from the Kerry fans.

Going into the game, I knew we'd do a good job setting the tone. We had let Cork set the tone for us before. We'd just walked out on to the pitch and waited to see what they had to offer. Darragh set the mood this time. He horsed into Nicholas Murphy from the start. And Galvin! Galvin was awesome. His best display ever of winning breaking ball. He was wired to the moon with passion. At one stage Galvin won four or five breaking balls in a row, driving in like a demented man. I don't know what page Joe Brolly occupies in the black book, but thanks, Joe.

Galvin and Darragh are at the centre of everything. Darragh would have seen what was written all summer about his clashes with Nicholas Murphy as a big motivation and challenge for the third game. He tore into it like a man possessed. He physically dominated Nicholas Murphy and wore him down in the end.

One incident before half-time almost scared me. There was a loose ball out on the sideline, Darragh burst to it, won it and turned. Pierce O'Neill was in front of him, screening him, basketball-style. O'Neill was on his toes, ready to block Darragh's way in the event of a dummy or a sidestep or a swerve. Instead, Darragh ploughed into him, keeled him over. The referee gave a free against Darragh. A harmless free.

I was a couple of yards away and there was wildness in Darragh's eyes. I let a roar at him to calm down a bit. He was so fired up. I turned away and grinned to myself.

The backs conceded exactly five points in each half. Bang on the target. Donaghy was magnificent. With Graham Canty gone, they sent the midfielder Derek Kavanagh in to the full-back position. Donaghy ran riot. He only got a point himself, but between being fouled and laying the ball off he must have accounted for seven or eight more points. He's the story of the summer by now.

Morgan was bitching before and after the game about the way we played. No grace. It's over, Billy. Grow up and take your beating.

On Tuesday night in Killarney we're coming back, training for an All-Ireland final. I'm going to enjoy every second of the next month.

21

This was an enjoyable day.

Myself, Pat and Ger travelled to Croke Park to watch the Dubs play Mayo in the other semi-final. You can't really settle down to preparing for an All-Ireland final till the other semi-final is decided and all the cards are on the table.

The Dubs threw it away in a style that will haunt them. There was some *ruaille buaille* beforehand. Mayo came out and ran down to the Hill 16 end to warm up. We're up in the stand and we're laughing away. What'll happen next? I'm thinking if Caffrey has any sense, he'll come out and pay no attention. Take his boys to the Canal end and use it to wind them up during the warm-up. In Killarney against Cork we lost the battle, but we made sure that we won the war. Caffrey should have said, let them have that little battle, boys. Let's go win the war.

Instead, the Dubs come out and do probably the worst thing they can do. They go to the Hill end themselves and make a half-hearted attempt to move Mayo out of the way. Caffrey gives John Morrison an embarrassing dunt in the back.

Still! The Dubs manage to get seven points up, fifteen minutes into the second half, and my notebook is full of stuff about how they play. We're already talking about how we will handle Conal Keaney and Alan Brogan. We're looking at Brogan in particular, asking each other who the Christ will we put on him. Marc Sé, we think. He'd know him from colleges football.

Next thing, though, Dublin let it all slip away. I can only think that some of the things they did in the second half were in preparation for playing us. They brought Darren Magee on as blood sub for Ciaran Whelan, and when Whelan came back they left Magee on and moved Shane Ryan to wing back. I could see what they were thinking. Darren Magee had made a huge contribution in Killarney, throwing our fellas around like rag dolls. I think they wanted to see if they could get Magee enough match time to make him a runner for some part in the final. But the change upset their whole balance. Shane Ryan had been the absolute key to winning their own kick-outs all season and he was the best midfielder on the field, picking up all the pieces. They should have left him where he was.

With Magee and Whelan they had two very similar players in midfield with limited mobility, and Magee, lacking match fitness, started to tire late on. Meanwhile poor Shane Ryan found himself isolated in a one-on-one in the corner-back position and the Mayo sub Andy Moran put the ball past him for a goal. That's a rough thing to happen to a player in Croke Park if he's not prepared for it. Ryan has come in as maybe the best midfielder of the year and has ended up on his backside as Mayo put the ball in the net in front of the Hill.

I see a lot that's familiar in the problems Dublin have. Dublin's heads weren't right. The attitude wasn't there. They got to a certain stage and the players were thinking of playing Kerry. Their other big problem was the same as ours last year. They haven't been tested. Bryan Cullen, for instance. In the Westmeath game, Bryan had been standing in the centre-back position and Westmeath were haplessly kicking the ball down his throat. He was coming on to it and he looked fantastic.

But against Mayo, Bryan Cullen was pulled all around the place. Mayo will do anything but kick the ball, so there was nothing dropping into Cullen's house at all now, no loose ball to mop up. Brady was dragging him away, running at him. No more lord-of-the-manor football. No more standing back and looking like McGeeney as he comes out very strong, looking for the pass.

The Dubs have this thing going where they think they are getting strength from the Hill. Before the match they do this routine of marching down towards the Hill, linking arms. They're ignoring all the other Dubs in the place, including most of their friends and family in the stands, but they think they are being empowered. To me it looks phoney and orchestrated.

If I ever told our fellas to do it, they wouldn't anyway. It comes across as contrived. I'm not even into this thing of clapping the supporters. I was as high as a kite after we beat Armagh last week. After the post-match interview I was coming back across the pitch. Cork were on next and, as I ran, the Kerry lads were going mad in the stand. I had this great urge to let a few roars out of me and shake a fist up to them, I was feeling so high. But I had to tell myself that it wasn't my way. I kept the head down and kept walking. Ran into the dressing room to the celebrations behind closed doors.

Maybe Dubs are just different. But this was the day they realized there's nothing coming back to them from the Hill. Any yahoo can support a team when it is going well. We discovered that in Kerry this year.

By the end Dublin had lost their whole shape. They didn't seem to understand the few simple things which make them tick. Mayo just threw the handle after the hatchet and played their best football coming to the finish. Ciarán McDonald kicked an unbelievable last point. Conor Mortimer played well. But deep down we know that Dublin would have been a tougher proposition for the final. Physically they were the only team that had given us bother, and they had brought a lot of flow and power into their attacking – they created five goal chances. Mayo have too much baggage to carry to a final. On their day we know they can cut loose, but when Pat, Ger and myself leave Croke Park, we feel without saying as much that there is an All-Ireland there for the taking if we finish the year doing the right things.

Mayo winning makes everything about the run to the final different. It's a different game now. I'm delighted when I see the papers the next day. There's any number of pundits saying that Dublin and Mayo was the greatest game ever played. It wasn't, of course. It was full of errors and loose football, but it was an exciting game. Mayo will buy into it all, anyway. It's been a huge event for them and, the more the semi-final gets talked up, the more the pressure switches to them. I always think you're better getting into a final with some dour old semi-final that you win by seven points to five, a game that everyone forgets instantly.

I know that if Dublin had made the final, they would have shut up shop. Caffrey wouldn't have talked. His team wouldn't have talked either. Their set-up is to say as little as possible. I think for them it's a mistake. The pressure-cooker situation is there. The media are mad for stories about Dublin. The Dubs say nothing, so the media start making up stories or inflating any little thing, and fellas are looking around the camp wondering who's to blame for this or that. Dublin need to learn to ride with it. We've learned that slowly. Armagh and Tyrone talk to anyone and they put these great myths out about themselves. Loughnane did it in Clare. Told everyone over and over again about running up that hill and the flaking they gave each other in training. For a couple of years everyone playing Clare was wondering about these lunatics who got up at dawn and ran up and down hills carrying each other on their backs. Wouldn't have been half as effective if they'd told nobody about it.

Dublin should give the media bits and pieces, promote themselves, use it to their advantage.

If Dublin had qualified for the final, I had planned to exploit their paranoia and use the media to turn the heat on them a bit. Now I decide that's definitely what we are going to do with Mayo. We'll be talking up the blondies, Mortimer and McDonald, ratcheting up the pressure. Slowly, slowly.

In all the excitement after the Dublin game Mayo are doing plenty of talking about being one big family, about their style of play, about how you'll never see a Mayo back just kicking the ball away, they like to work it out. It's like giving us a list of things we should work on!

22

The last lap starts on Monday, 28 August. Another night in Fitz-gerald Stadium. A large number of the usual kafflers watching like crows from their seats in the stand. An easy session goes a bit off-kilter when the drug-testers arrive. They have their business to do, but the session is fairly distracted – and it gets worse when Aidan O'Mahony runs into somebody and gets three teeth knocked out. Brendan Guiney is also injured. Sean Walsh is wan-dering around with a folder, getting little bits and pieces of infor-mation for the Press Night. There's just too much going on. We're not focused. We need to cut the peripheral stuff after tonight.

Mahony finds two of his teeth in the grass. The whole lot of us are enlisted to help him find the other one. Ger says we should use the system for finding golf balls where everyone proceeds in a line, so we all go on hands and knees, crawling up and down, looking for Mahony's tooth. The old lads in the stand think we're either praying to Allah or practising a new style of forward training. We can't find the third tooth, anyway. It doesn't bother Mahony too much. It's not the first blow he's taken this year. He gets shipped off to the dentist for damage limitation.

He'll soldier on. We need to get focused.

For a few sessions we hold the team back from full-out foot-ball. Zones. Drills. Intensity work. We want them back to feeling hungry for some football.

On Saturday, 2 September, we organize a full-scale match in the stadium. Aodán MacGearailt injures his metatarsal. The poor man is jinxed with injuries. We put Declan on the forty for the 'A' team and Eoin on the forty for the 'B' team. The 'A's beat the 'B's by 2–17 to 2–11. It's very competitive. Declan does well. Brossy does well.

Afterwards we talk about the possibility of playing Brossy at wing forward. Seán O'Sullivan is not going great right now. There is a rumour going around that Mayo may play Patrick Harte at ten. Brosnan could help Tomás Ó Sé on that side, if he was on Harte, who is a midfielder.

This is going to be the toughest decision of our three years together. I say to Johnny, Ger and Pat that we must make the decision on Declan on the basis of what we see in front of our eyes at training. After that I couldn't give a damn if we are a part of a tiny minority in the county. I talk to the selectors and say we have to be ruthless, we have to be emotionally detached. The boys would know that this decision will be huge for me emotionally. They nod and say the right things.

Complicating matters is the business of the captaincy. In Kerry it seems to matter more than in most places who gets to actually lift the cup. When Dromid won the South Kerry championship in 2004 and South Kerry won the county championship, it meant that Dromid could nominate Declan as county captain for the next year. The following winter, Valentia won the South Kerry championship, South Kerry retained the county title and Valentia kindly let Declan continue as captain.

With Declan off the team, however, the honour of captaining falls to the beaten county finalists, Dr Crokes of Killarney. Gooch has been captaining the side since Declan was dropped. He's popular and coming back into form, and in Killarney it is known that if Declan is picked, Crokes will not just see Eoin maybe dropped from the team but the Gooch will lose the captaincy.

This is one omelette that isn't going to get made without breaking a lot of eggs.

The easy decision might be to leave well enough alone for peace sake. Picking Declan will lead to huge bitterness in Killarney. Very few things about Killarney this summer make me likely to shy off another confrontation, though. The rumour mill has had its day. It's between players now.

The whole tone of the debate and the attitude of the Killarney gang rankles. If Eoin is the best centre-forward in the county, why do Crokes play him just about everywhere except centre-forward?

A few weeks ago the *Sunday Indo* ran a piece that was a compilation of some of the rumours which have been going around. I don't know where most of the stuff came from, but I was disappointed to see Pat O'Shea, the Crokes manager, was quoted in there. He should have stayed out of it, but he was quoted as saying we were playing a style alien to Kerry.

A football man should know the story better than anyone about having a go. At the time he was referring to, Donaghy was still a midfielder. The ball just wasn't sticking inside with the full-forward line, and the lads outside were carrying it and just trying to play it a bit cuter. If Pat O'Shea had looked at how we played when we had Crowley, we'd lamped it in from everywhere. The point is, you play the style according to the players you have. Pat doesn't use Eoin Brosnan as a centre-forward because he needs him elsewhere.

That's the basic fact of the matter. The players you have dictate the style, and Pat, whose Dr Crokes teams play a more hand-passing and running system themselves, should have thought of that before pontificating about alien styles.

To me, Declan O'Sullivan is the best centre-forward in Kerry. He certainly went through a patch this year where he was burned out, when he looked overplayed. That's my own fault. The last few seasons, Kerry have gone to the All-Ireland each September and things have gone well after that for South Kerry and for Dromid. Declan has played all those games. The local championship final usually gets played the week before Christmas. It's madness for a county player to be playing games of that intensity so late in the year and then be back in for training in January and playing the McGrath Cup at the end of January.

There's several things at work here. I can't play favourites. I can't punish Declan because I'm afraid of being seen to play favourites.

We'll make the right decision, but before we do I'll walk up many the side of many a hill saying, 'C'mon you bastard, take your heart out of it.'

The players have to be happy with the motives for making the decision. If they think it's an honest decision they'll move on. If they think we selectors are worrying about how it will look, there will be trouble. I won't go myself and ask any player's opinion, but I'm using Ger as the fly on the wall. Johnny and Pat as well if they get the chance.

Declan started on the 'A' team in Killarney on form. Eoin Brosnan had a poor enough game in the semi-final against Cork. According to the stats he touched the ball six times in fifty minutes or so. Declan came on and touched it eight times in the last twenty minutes. That doesn't make Eoin a bad player, it just reflects a bit of change in form.

It's no secret that Declan and I are clubmates (we're even distant relatives) and we have been close, but I've never had a problem with Eoin. He scores a lot of goals and likes to shoot for goal. At one stage in the run to the final, a rumour came to me that there was a betting scene going on in Killarney that revolves around Eoin scoring goals. Somebody said to me that Brossy hasn't kicked a point in training for two months. It's bullshit, but typical of what has been going on around the team.

Eoin is a very decent, very quiet guy. No matter what way I go on this though, fellas will see it as a conspiracy. If Declan is picked, it will be that South Kerry cute hoor getting his 'son' on the team. Some haydog of a journalist wrote a piece around the time of the Munster final. In a moment of emotion I had said once in 2004 what a night it would be if Declan ever arrived back down to Dromid with the Sam Maguire. This quote (helpfully supplied by a Kerryman) was the introduction to the article, the general thrust of which was this: Jack O'Connor is a misguided manager who can't see past his own nose and his own patch.

Now if I leave Declan off, it will be said that I was cowed by that sort of stuff.

I'd like to spend two months out in solitude in a beehive hut on the Skelligs, just mulling this one over, but on the first Monday in September we have the All-Ireland Press Night.

Bryan Sheehan calls me the night before. He needs to talk urgently. It's so urgent, he'll take a day off to do it. So we meet in the old Ringside Rest Hotel when I finish teaching in Bryan's old school at lunchtime.

Bryan and myself go a long way back through the Mhuirí Cup teams for Coláiste na Sceilge. We're at ease around each other, which is probably why he lays all his cards on the table now. He feels he's not getting a fair crack of the whip. He's going well in training, playing on Tommy Griffin. He has a conspiracy theory. He thinks that I'm not putting him on because he'd have to be the Kerry captain ahead of Declan.

Aw fuck. He's getting all this stuff in his ear around Cahirciveen. That's how bad and corrosive it is. People in South Kerry are turning on each other, playing a fella from Cahirciveen off a fella from a few miles up the road in Dromid.

Bryan's case is straightforward enough. He came on against Armagh for ten minutes and did well. He missed out altogether on the Cork game through injury. He didn't even travel. He's not realistically in line for a start right now. He's had no competitive game for two months, but this is in his ear every time he goes out in Cahirciveen.

We have a frank exchange. I ask Bryan to withdraw the comment or the meeting is over.

On a busy day I could have done without this. Bryan is a very talented footballer. Sometimes we want more from him in terms of aggression, though. There's nothing that would give me more pleasure now than to tell my old pupil that he'll be starting the All-Ireland final. But I can't.

My year of part-time teaching is over now. I'm back to school after lunch with Bryan. Then up to Killarney for a one-on-one interview for a newspaper. Then to the pitch, where we hold a session for an hour and a half.

Then I do a couple of photo things with cameras, and we head to the Brehon Hotel for a bit of grub. Then into the press room with the lot of us. I do four TV interviews. Three one-on-one pieces with papers. Then take general questions for thirty minutes with twenty journalists.

Before we go into the press room I give about five minutes'

media coaching to the lads. Simple stuff. Lads, we can use this to our advantage. Turn up the bit of heat on the Mayo fellas, pinpoint a few key players. Ye've nothing to be afraid of. Ye're brighter than most of the fellas down there with pens and tape recorders. You know more about football than they do. Go down, enjoy it. We'll all go together. We won't pick victims to throw to them this year, we'll spread the burden. Say nothing stupid. Any Mayo players you want to talk about, choose the fellas with blond hair.

Our job is made easy. Journalists are keen to inflate Mayo after the Dublin game. They're still blowing the froth off the greatest game ever. We've had our dour old game with Cork, and Morgan has come out with a few yards of the reliable guff about how dirty and cynical we are. The media are doing our job for us.

As I sit in a chair, towards the end of a long day, I'm surrounded by journalists and cameras. I notice the Gooch is in one corner, surrounded in exactly the same way. And Donaghy is in another corner, entertaining them all the while. I should be worried but what the hell, it's all in the pot now.

23

In training, Eoin is on the forty on the 'A' team and Declan on the other forty on the 'B' team. We switch things as much as we can, and at one stage we have a half-forward line of Seán O'Sullivan, Eoin and Darren O'Sullivan playing on the 'A' backs. The thing isn't working. We stand watching and there in front of us we can see. It's not fucking working. Bryan Sheehan and Paddy Kelly are tearing into our 'A' midfield and the half-forward line aren't able to rescue them.

It's an important scenario for us to see. Eoin Brosnan is a tremendous player when you are on top in midfield. He's not a man to go back and link. If you win primary ball, he'll come on to it like a train when you pop it in front of him.

Declan O'Sullivan is a great man to link the play, to know when to slip a pass and keep it going. And he's coming into form.

For the weekend before the All-Ireland we decide to head back to Cork. Our season turned with that weekend in the Hayfield Manor and we'll head back there for a night after a full-scale practice game in Páirc Uí Chaoimh.

For training games we pick the match-ups very carefully. You need to be bringing the best out of players in training games and trials. Get players who will put it up to each other.

The final trial game in Páirc Uí Chaoimh is an event for the players. Five days before the game, my phone rings. Brendan Guiney on the line. Brendan is one of my guys, a fine, tough footballer. Every panel needs a Brendan Guiney on it. I've never seen anybody as dedicated as Brendan – he missed one session all year, winter or summer. If we ever need to check out a forward in training, we send him in beside Guiney. Tells us all we need to know about a forward when we see him beside a genuine tough customer. There's a grand mad streak in Brendan, which is good for a defender. Any forward going in to him wasn't going to get it easy any night.

Brendan broke his wrist early on in a college game this year and, although he's been with us all the way through, he hasn't played a minute with Kerry in the league or championship this season. He's not just a fine footballer but a desperate, hungry one.

'Who am I marking?' he says.

'Paul Galvin.'

'Sound.'

I know what I'm doing here. Apart from the positions matching up, Galvin and Guiney are from keen rival clubs in North Kerry, Listowel and Finuge. I want the last session to have some edge to it.

One evening not long ago, anyone watching from the stand in Fitzgerald Stadium would have seen Tommy Griffin marking Darragh and Tommy flaking into Darragh. In the league game in Tyrone we were hammering them at one stage and in the second half they upped the ante and twice in the second half Darragh got bowled over by fuckers not half his size. So I said to him a few times to expect that we'd up the ante inside in training.

Guys were giving him too much respect. For his own sake, fellas were going to have to start laying into the likes of him. We weren't playing our football at a high enough intensity level in training. So if there was a fella playing on Darragh in training, I'd tell him to skelp him a few times. Usually that would be Tommy. Darragh got a bit offended one evening, and himself and Tommy threw a couple of flakes at each other.

I went to Tommy afterwards and just said, 'Tommy, I want more of that.' Tommy just said, 'Fair enough.' I didn't speak to Darragh. I didn't mollycoddle him or put the arm around him or tell him not to worry. I was in cahoots with Tommy. We wanted that edge.

When we get to Páirc Uí Chaoimh, we put Eoin Brosnan in midfield with Darragh to start. By now Declan has more or less nailed the centre-forward place. There's no need to say to Eoin that centre-forward is gone. To be honest, with the way he's regaining his form, Declan is making himself undroppable. Eoin goes to midfield on the 'A' team. Now Tommy Griffin is the one under pressure. I go to Tommy and tell him, 'Don't be under any illusions here today, your spot is under severe pressure.'

So Brosnan and Griffin go head to head. Brosnan starts well. After about ten minutes of play, we have to stop. Galvin and Guiney are rolling around on the ground, throwing punches at each other. Brian White, who I've invited over from Wexford to referee the game, is standing over the two brawling Kerrymen, screaming at them.

'Stop that! Stop that, lads! Ye'll be sent off for that in an All-Ireland final.'

I'm on the sideline when I catch Darragh Ó Sé's eye. We have to turn away from each other with our heads down. Our shoulders are shaking with laughter. This is perfect.

In midfield, Tommy comes into it late. We're looking for fire. Darragh has to go off for the last ten minutes, and when Tommy moves on to the 'A' team he shows a real bit of that. Determination. Bloody-mindedness.

It's tight. In the end Tommy is a better foil for Darragh Ó Sé. Poor Eoin has lost out on two counts. There had been a chance of getting in at wing forward in place of Seán O'Sullivan, but Seán has played well and in our hearts we know that Eoin is a central player. He needs to be up and down the centre of the field.

I know that Eoin being dropped is going to play badly in Killarney. My worries are for Eoin, though. He's very quiet and a bit hard to reach and I would like to think I have a good relationship with him, but we wouldn't be as close as we could be. I know the decision will hurt him. I don't want that, and I don't want him to be in the wrong frame of mind for the final either. We'll need him at some stage.

As for Crokes themselves, Declan's return means they are losing the captaincy as well. A hard blow for any club, especially one as proud as Dr Crokes. What goes around, though. Back in 2001,

Crokes weren't a bit shy about pushing for Eoin to take the captaincy off Seamus Moynihan in the run-up to the catastrophe against Meath. Seamus was a legend and Eoin was just making his way into the team. He'd played one and a half championship games when Crokes decided to invoke their right to the captaincy for the first game of the year in Croke Park. Any bellyaching will be a bit rich if it comes from Crokes.

On Tuesday evening I pull Eoin aside out on the field and tell him our decision before the training starts. You can see in a man's body language that you've hit him hard. By the end of the week there'll be stories, of course, that Eoin stormed out of training. Sounds good, but not true.

That evening was a kiddies' night, where a lot of children came down to watch training and the players were signing autographs for them as they came in and out. I'm out on the field, having a couple of kicks with a few lads staying out late. I see Eoin go in to get changed back into his clothes. He makes a beeline out the side gate to avoid the crowd and leaves out across the small pitch behind the stadium.

I have no problem in the world with that. If it were myself, I'd have climbed out over the walls and run.

Eoin doesn't come down for the meal afterwards. Who could blame him?

I'd asked him if he wanted to go out for a bit of grub, discuss it. No, he'd said, it's fine.

He didn't have to tell me any more. It was written on his face.

He told me later that he was very down for a couple of days. In that time I was dying to talk with him, but I said I'd leave him alone and take my chance for a quiet word up in Dublin.

One of the joys when we pick the team for the final is that there isn't much debate about picking Mike Frank Russell. It only struck me during the summer when I saw it working. For Mike Frank to flourish you need a Donaghy or a Crowley in there.

In 2004 he made way for Crowley. The next year we dropped him because we couldn't make him into a Crowley. This year, feeding off Donaghy, he looks himself again, a gifted player, a beautiful kicker, a finisher.

Every player has an image of himself as a certain type of player. A ball-winner. A finisher. A playmaker. A creator. Franny would see himself as an assassin. I'd been trying to make the full package out of him, looking for things out of Mike Frank that he couldn't deliver. He's a finisher, an artist. He's not a John Crowley. He's a different type of player. I was trying to get him to tackle and stand his ground and to hit haymakers. Not his game. He's an assassin.

There's another gem I pulled from Brian Clough's autobiography years ago. Clough said that you should never try to get a man to do what he's not capable of because you'll destroy him. I made that mistake with Mike Frank. I put my hand up and say I was at least partly to blame. He'll always be one of the players who will say he didn't get a fair crack off me, but his turn has come around again and I'm glad. I hope we're okay with each other now.

Anyway, we picked the team and told the players.

1. Diarmuid Murphy
2. Marc Ó Sé
3. Michael McCarthy
4. Tom O'Sullivan
5. Tomás Ó Sé
6. Seamus Moynihan
7. Aidan O'Mahony
8. Darragh Ó Sé
9. Tommy Griffin
10. Seán O'Sullivan
11. Declan O'Sullivan (captain)
12. Paul Galvin
13. Colm Cooper
14. Kieran Donaghy
15. Mike Frank Russell

Even in a good year, when the decisions are straightforward you put your selection out there and brace yourself for some reaction.

No matter how gently you tread, you've walked on a few dreams in picking an All-Ireland team. I know the tug of emotion that was there when we thought seriously about dropping Declan. That's replicated everywhere.

Training on that Tuesday was at half past six. Word of the team travelled fast. At five past nine, when I was driving home, I heard the beeping of the mobile. Here we go.

'You should be ashamed of yourself by upsetting a winning team. Hope it backfires on you. And I mean it.'

The words hit me across the face like a good haymaker. I don't recognize the number but the text has come so quickly after the end of training that I know it can't be coming from anyone too far away from the heart of the team. For the entire drive home to Finan's Bay I keep glancing at the text. It hurts.

I get home, shaken. Wounded. Everyone is up, but eventually Bean an Tí drifts up to bed. I fetch one of the boys' mobile phones and ring the number on loudspeaker. 'Hello?'

The hair stands up on the back of my neck when I hear the voice. I expected some flack from up Killarney way, but this is from inside the camp. The voice belongs to the close relative of one of the team. I realize straight away too when I hear the voice that the text wasn't meant to be sent anonymously. The sender would have assumed that I would have the number.

I was better off not knowing. I've made a mistake in wanting to find out. It's just a bad, bad thing, knowing where the text came from. A knife through me.

My father has been in Dublin only once. That was to visit my mother in hospital. As it happened, a neighbour was in hospital in Dublin too at the time, and my father was able to benefit from a lift to the city.

The neighbour had been catching fish while everyone was at Mass on a Sunday morning. There was a quick way to poach back then, if you could get your hands on some dynamite. You just blew up a little section of lake, and soon the fish would float to the top. Our neighbour was in a hurry and the dynamite blew before he was ready. The poor man was badly damaged. And mixed with the pain was always this thing over dynamiting fish when everyone was at Mass. People understood, but there was a judgement in their voice when they said it. They used a whisper to tell how it happened.

I feel a bit like my old neighbour when I read the text. People will be whispering. He picked his own man to lift the cup. That's how it is. And it hurts.

24

On days when the solitude of Skellig Michael beckons, I think of my old headmaster, Con Dineen, and the dog Latin phrase he'd use in relation to troublesome pupils. *Noli Sinere Bastardis Carborundum Est!* Fair enough, Con boy. I won't let the bastards grind me down!

We move on.

On the morning of the All-Ireland I called Declan up to the room. I said to him, 'Don't feel as though I did you a favour. You worked for your place. Go out and play your game, and fuck the rest of them.'

Easy words. Can I say of myself that I didn't give a damn? Not really. Of course winning the All-Ireland with Declan captaining the team would be the icing on the cake for a man who had made the long journey from Dromid to Croker; but if I thought picking him might cost us the All-Ireland, I wouldn't have picked him.

I think we made the right choice, but the text over the team selection reminds me of what else is out there. When I stopped hurting and being annoyed over it, I got to seeing it from the sender's point of view.

The GAA isn't just about what happens on the pitch, it reaches right into the heart of the country like nothing else does. Jer O'Shea taught me that. Maurice Fitz taught me, too. It is something that reaches into homes. The text is another reminder. We are dealing with people's lives here.

It's not about kissing the crest or wrapping yourself in the green and gold. It's something more fundamental. It's about blood and soil.

One day before we made the decision and I was in real turmoil about it, I went as usual for a long walk up Toorsaleen. Being home and thinking the whole thing through reminded me of a work by a Kerry man. Old John B. Keane. Something clicked in my head. We were doing *The Field* in school with a junior cert, class and we had watched the movie. There's a scene in the film where Richard Harris goes into the presbytery and the priest is inside with the Yank. The priest has taken the Yank's side and the Bull is mad.

An eviction notice has been served to him on presbytery notepaper.

The cattle will be put out. The Bull starts ranting and raving, telling the Yank that if he knows what's good for him he'll get out of the town. He starts telling a story then and getting a bit misty-eyed. He's trying to get across to the priest and the Yank what it meant to him, that field. He says that one day he was bringing in the hay, himself and his father, and the word came that his mother had died, just keeled over and died.

The father says to the son, 'Look, we'll have to bring in the hay before it rains.' The Bull gets fiercely emotional. That's how much the field meant to his father. Blood and tears. He said to them that if they thought the Bull McCabe would face his mother in heaven and not fight for that field, they'd have something else coming to them.

And a part of me was walking on Toorsaleen up above my father's place and looking towards Glencar, towards a mountain that my mother and Declan's mother grew up on either side of, and I was thinking the same sort of thoughts. I don't want to sound too dramatic, but I muttered to myself that if them fuckers who'd been stirring it and whispering all summer thought I'd face my mother in heaven without giving Declan O'Sullivan his fair shot at captaining his county, they were very much mistaken.

That's how much it meant to me. It meant as much to me as the field meant to the Bull.

It meant as much to my text correspondent as well. I know that now. That's why we love the game and play the game. That's why it's different. Everything else is mixed up in it. Life and death. Blood and soil.

'Johneen *a chroí*, don't take that job at all, they'll be giving out to you,' my mother said to me with her last words. She didn't know football but she knew what it meant in Kerry. Religion causes fewer rows.

We are having our team talk in the hotel the night before the All-Ireland. We have this routine for Dublin games now where we go out to Westmanstown, in Clonsilla, Co. Dublin, and have a kick-around the night before a game. We go up on the train, as Kerry teams always have, check into our hotel and then head out for a few kicks, a stretch, a small chat in the corner of the field for five minutes just to set the tone. Back for grub, then a team meeting.

The meeting back in the hotel is in my own bedroom. I've asked for the biggest suite in Dunboyne Castle for this reason. They've given me a big suite in the corner. I want to do something different.

So we get the starting team in and tell them each very specifically what we want. We have told Eoin to come along. And Eamon Fitz. Eamon is just a very solid guy, a great leader and talker, and he adds something to any meeting. I want to make Eoin feel part of the thing. No matter what you do, though, it's hard for subs to feel as much a part of it as you would want them.

We go through everything. The guys are relaxed and happy. Not having the meeting in a proper meeting room makes a difference. The atmosphere is very together. It's been a long, long road. Most of the guys in the room were on the Kerry team before I became manager. They were pilloried and laughed at in the weeks after bad defeats. They kept giving it their all.

I think Eoin is good with things. Nobody wanted to see him lose out, but within the team I think the lads know that Declan had played his way back in. Somebody was going to suffer.

The Gooch seems good, too. When the captaincy went, there was no reaction from the Gooch. Just like when it was handed to him. He handles things his own quiet way because he's been doing that since he burst through as a kid. He's learned to take things as they come.

I mentioned it to him before the Press Night that he would be asked questions about the captaincy. We agree that the best thing to say would be, 'Look, I'm captain now, but there's no guarantees about the All-Ireland final.' At that stage, Declan was shaping up and it looked like he could be on team.

One evening at training I ran a couple of laps with him, conveniently, just to get into his ear. Maybe deep down he's disappointed, but he doesn't show it. Those around him, club and family, are probably more disappointed. He's rooming as usual with Declan, and I think between them there'll be nothing different. Like the rest of the team this weekend is about being there for each other.

We talk for a while as a group in the room. We had a meeting like this the first year I was manager, and I went to Declan Coyle beforehand for advice on something. Declan said to go ahead, so I'd told the team that I was sure they were going to win the next day. Sure and positive.

I don't want to say the same thing again. It's something you only ever say to a team once, but I am sure we will win the All-Ireland final. If everything I believe about things balancing out in the long road is true, then we will win.

We close the meeting with the usual reminders. Sleep well. Hydrate. Switch off the mobile phones and leave them. Meet for breakfast. Ferocious togetherness, guys.

We go our separate ways with just seventy minutes of football left to be played in this long, mad year.

Eoin is still on my mind when I get up the next morning. I want him positive and tuned in. I send him a text to call up to the room. He never arrives. It's a distraction. Fuck, I think, he's thick with me.

It's true maybe that you'd only be softening the blow by telling a fella he'll be playing a huge part, but in Eoin's case it will be true. It's more than that, though. It's all about keeping the chemistry right in the squad. If one fella is thick with you, it snowballs. Even on All-Ireland day. It runs through a team like a shiver. You are constantly keeping the balance right. That's why you go out of your way to touch base with certain fellas.

On the way back from Mass in Dunboyne I make it my business to single Eoin out. We walk up the road on our own.

'Be positive, Eoin, it'll work out for you.'

He tells me it's okay. He has his mind made up to be positive. He's over the initial disappointment and he's fine.

Fantastic. I don't raise the issue of him not coming to the room. (It dawns on me later that I have ordered them all to leave their phones off.)

In the afternoon, Eoin comes on and kicks 1−1 from the middle of the field.

Everything works.

We identified small areas that made Mayo tick and luckily they hadn't changed them for the final. Their kick-outs we identified as being a key area. The Ballina connection. Four Ballina players around the middle and a Ballina goalie.

Our players got very into this. We have noticed too that Mayo's big ploy is to hit the wing-back spot. If the kick-out is going to the right-hand side, Gardiner, say, would make a run across field, vacating the position and bringing his marker with him. The midfielder McGarrity would run into the space Gardiner had just left. We decided that the wing forward would just stay put and not follow Gardiner at all. The goalie would look up and there would be no hole to aim for. We won nine of their first twelve kick-outs.

The other big one we emphasized was to put huge heat on them coming out of defence. Mayo prided themselves on slipping passes to fellas running off each other's shoulders.

They never varied it. We worked for weeks before the All-Ireland at hitting them there.

And we kept them busy. If you are always hitting the long ball in, the opposition half-backs are going to cheat by dropping back. So you have to get your half-forwards on the ball to keep their half-backs honest. We would have been big on the short punched pass slipped to the half-forward to draw the half-back out so they couldn't crowd Gooch and the boys.

And we did a lot on our own kick-outs and the type of ball to the inside line, encouraging Seamus Moynihan to come on to the ball and kick it early and diagonally.

And we varied it. When we'd looked back on the Cork game, we saw that we were putting too much high ball in to Donaghy. Joe Brolly had said that we had two tactics. Kick it in high to Kieran Donaghy. Or kick it in even higher. Not far off the truth.

Look at our first goal in the final, though. Tommy Griffin catching a ball and punching it out to Seán O'Sullivan. Seán Bán is blocked off, so he throws it out to Moynihan, and in the one move Moynihan hits a lovely fifty-yard pass across the field to the Gooch, who came off his man as soon as Moynihan got the ball. In one movement Gooch transfers it into the middle to Declan, who is coming like a train. There's a one–two played between himself and Donaghy, and Declan puts it in the net. First goal of the game, and effectively it's over.

Everything works. For once it's not a game of inches.

Donaghy got a great route-one goal off Tommy Griffin. Seamus Moynihan came through for a point. It was a celebration.

We'd changed. I'd changed. When the Gooch got a clip early in the second half from the Mayo wing-back, Aidan Higgins, we knew what to do. Donaghy wasn't long going in and sorting him for retribution. I'd told him that was to happen. I said I didn't ever again want to to see the Gooch isolated if he is after getting a flake. Against Tyrone last year I said the opposite, and nobody protected us. That can be seen in whatever terms people like, but it's reality. If the officials won't take action, players are forced to settle things for themselves.

When it was over Declan went up the steps to lift the cup. He brought his friend the Gooch with him. That's the picture. The two of them lifting the Sam Maguire. Two young men who've been through harder things than football brought a bit of grace and perspective to us all.

Often in a season you are just a victim of circumstance. You do what you can, but events carry you along. We had our trials and tribulations, our hurts and our tears, but things came full circle. Darragh got a deserved All-Star award and in most people's eyes was Player of the Year. Dara Ó Cinnéide (along with Tony O'Keeffe and Fergus Clifford) watched the All-Ireland final for us from high in the stands as our eyes in the sky. And in the end we won an All-Ireland playing Kerry football after all. After a spring and half a summer worrying about the dark art of the tackle, we came out and won by playing catch and kick. The Kerry way! It came back to the old thing of finding a man who can stand his ground near the enemy goal. A target man.

Most of this year we have been in the discomfort zone, but, for a team, that isn't a bad place to be. You have everyone energized. Everyone thinking. Everyone wondering about getting straightened out.

There's no plan or blueprint. You go with what your gut tells you. You'll be paralysed if you think of the consequences.

We travel home with the bad days forgotten. Winning erases everything.

Travelling south on the train with the big canister in the vanguard. My happy conversation is interrupted by the familiar bleep of the mobile; text from a certain player somewhere down the carriage.

'Remember this text, Jack? "Tom, You will regret not returning my call. I want no casual footballers in my squad. If you don't think it worth your while to return my call you can fuck off. J." From the man who held Conor Mortimer scoreless and saved your job!'

Last laugh to my buddy, Tom O'Sullivan. Fucking rogue!

In the early hours of Tuesday morning in the Gleneagle Hotel outside Killarney, Declan and I met in the middle of a long corridor, half asleep and half drunk. That night we would bring the cup to our desolate old home place of Dromid and we both knew it would mean more than words to be there.

So we met and we had a bit of an embrace. There was nothing

to be said, not after all we had been through from Dromid to Coláiste na Sceilge to Croke Park and home again. Jer O'Shea was with us along the way, my mother, Oliver Walsh and Mike Cooper and many, many more. How can you describe those things?

September closes the circles. Declan and Gooch on the steps. Seeing Jer's sister Martina at the homecoming in Cahirciveen. The cup coming to Dromid, to the community and the community centre that football built. Tears in my eyes as I speak there about the whole long journey.

In the corridor Declan shook his head. He said, 'That was some fucking risk we took there.'

It was only hitting him then that if it hadn't worked we'd all have been run out of town by men with torches and pikes!

'Some risk, man,' Declan said again.

It was. Every summer championship is Russian roulette. Only one survives. In Kerry we are good at it. Because in Kerry, in South Kerry especially, we are born to survive.

Acknowledgments

My wife Bridie and sons Cian and Eanna are top of the list when it comes to thanking people. They could write their own book on what it's like to live with an inter-county manager. At times it's far from easy.

Thanks also to my family in Toorsaleen for their support. My father, who is eighty-nine, is the toughest, hardest-working man I've ever known. Himself and my late mother were amazingly resilient people who gave us everything they ever had.

To the three men who soldiered with me through good times and bad, Pat Flanagan, Johnny Culloty and Ger O'Keeffe. Thanks also to the backroom team who helped make Kerry the most professional Gaelic football team in the country.

I will be forever indebted to the three men who gave me my shot at the big time: Sean Walsh, Eamonn O'Sullivan and Jerome Conway.

A big thank-you to all the Kerry players who bounced back from adversity and took Gaelic football to another level in September 2006 in Croke Park.

The Dromid Pearses club is one of the smallest clubs in the country, but they have the biggest heart and spirit imaginable. It was the vision and resilience of people like their chairman of thirty years, Jeremiah O'Shea, who kept the dream alive.

A big thank-you to Michael Donnelly, Principal of Coláiste na Sceilge, and all the staff for their help and support over the past few years.

Special thanks also to Martina O'Shea for her bravery and generosity.

My old buddy, Jerry Mahony, was always an outlet for me when I wanted to get things off my chest. He never told me what I wanted to hear, but his advice has stood the test of time. Thanks, Jerry.

Thanks also to Gerard and Patricia Kennedy in The Bridge Bar (and Moorings Guesthouse) in Portmagee for all their hospitality, especially when this book was being written.

Without the promptings of Michael McLoughlin of Penguin Ireland, this book would never have been conceived. Thanks also to Brendan Barrington for his patient and meticulous editing.

Finally a huge thank you to Tom Humphries for his patience and understanding. I know there were times when I must have nearly cracked him as he tried to make sense of all my ramblings. He has shown incredible intelligence in the way he weaved it all into an emotional and coherent story.

And to anyone else who helped along the way but isn't mentioned here due to pressures of space and bad memory, thanks also!

Index